Deemed 'the father of th
Austin Freeman had a lo
a writer of detective fiction. He was born in London, the son of a tailor who went on to train as a pharmacist. After graduating as a surgeon at the Middlesex Hospital Medical College, Freeman taught for a while and joined the colonial service, offering his skills as an assistant surgeon along the Gold Coast of Africa. He became embroiled in a diplomatic mission when a British expeditionary party was sent to investigate the activities of the French. Through his tact and formidable intelligence, a massacre was narrowly avoided. His future was assured in the colonial service. However, after becoming ill with blackwater fever, Freeman was sent back to England to recover and, finding his finances precarious, embarked on a career as acting physician in Holloway Prison. In desperation, he turned to writing and went on to dominate the world of British detective fiction, taking pride in testing different criminal techniques. So keen were his powers as a writer that part of one of his best novels was written in a bomb shelter.

BY THE SAME AUTHOR
ALL PUBLISHED BY HOUSE OF STRATUS

Flighty Phyllis

R Austin Freeman

HOUSE OF
STRATUS

This edition published in 2001 by House of Stratus, an imprint of
Stratus Books Ltd., 21 Beeching Park, Kelly Bray,
Cornwall, PL17 8QS, UK.

www.houseofstratus.com

Typeset, printed and bound by House of Stratus.

A catalogue record for this book is available from the British Library
and the Library of Congress.

ISBN 0-7551-0358-0

CONTENTS

FLIGHT ONE

The Understudy

I have been the victim of circumstances. That is to be quite clearly understood at the outset. I accept no responsibility whatever. A purely passive agent – if that is not a contradiction in terms – I have been borne unresisting on the stream of events.

Mind! I am not complaining of circumstances. On the whole they have provided quite a high-class entertainment. I am merely disclaiming responsibility for situations that were not of my own choosing.

The first link in the chain of circumstance was forged when old Dr. Lederbogen of Munich had my head shaved. The barbarian! Just think of it! All my beautiful silky hair mown off to make room for a beastly ice-bag. But it won't bear thinking of. Even now, my eyes fill at the recollection of that hideous tragedy.

Of course, I knew nothing about it at the time, being more or less delirious. And even when I recovered my wits, I didn't discover the horror immediately, for my head was enveloped in a German night-cap that looked like a large cutlet-frill; and though a cutlet-frill is not the most becoming head-dress in the world, still, a good deal depends on the cutlet. I wasn't dissatisfied when I looked in the glass. I only wondered how they had tucked my hair away so neatly.

But when that cap came off for the first time! My aunt! Old Lederbogen realized, if he never had before, the rich expressiveness

1

of the English language when combined judiciously with German expletives. The initial explosion fairly shot him out on the landing, and I heard him going down the stairs three at a time.

I won't attempt to say what my head looked like. You can take your choice between a hedgehog and a boot-brush. Mere language – printable language – is unequal to the occasion.

When I was quite recovered I shook off the dust of Munich. My voice, which I had come there to train, was pronounced by the expert – his very appropriate name was Haase – to be "too deep for a woman's and not strong enough for a man's." The rude old pig! He little knew – but I mustn't anticipate. I will only remark that the rich chest notes of my voice constituted circumstance number two.

Old Lederbogen had carefully kept my hair, I will say that for him, and before I left Munich I had it made up into a wig. Very cleverly the man did it, too, with a lot of fluffy, fringey arrangements round the edges to cover the join. It was a perfect success. No one would have suspected for an instant that it was not just ordinary hair. But it felt horrid, and, of course, I knew about the boot-brush underneath, if no one else did.

The next link in the chain of circumstance was forged by my cousin Charlie. I had written to him asking him to look out for a nice quiet bachelor flat for me, for I had just come in to my Uncle Alfred's property – about twelve hundred a year – and I meant to have a good time. Charlie wrote me a long letter in reply from which I quote the passage that bears on this tragic history.

"Concerning the flat that you speak about: I wonder how you would like my chambers in Clifford's Inn. They are a small set, but they are very cosy and exceedingly quiet. The best of the Inn is that you can come and go as you please without being noticed by anybody, and there is a night porter at the Fleet Street gate, so you don't need to trouble about what time you get home. There are plenty of women living in the Inn now, in fact the place is infested with them – that is why I am thinking of giving up my chambers. In any case, you had better try them for a few days and see if you like them. It will be better than going to an hotel. I have asked Mr Larkin, the head porter, to have the rooms got ready for you, and he will give you the key if you call at the lodge."

"I am sending you a ticket for a fancy-dress ball that the Chelsea models are giving to the artists and students. It will be quite in your line – a little bit boisterous but perfectly proper – and you may meet some of the fellows whom you used to see when you and I were working at the Slade School. I shall be there, but not in costume; one can't come up by train from Blackheath dressed as Punchinello or Mephistopheles. I shall wear ordinary evening clothes, but you must come in costume, and I will see you home to the Inn and you can tell me whether you care to take over the chambers from me. So adieu! until we meet at Chelsea."

That was the gist of Charlie's letter, and I may say at once that I was charmed with his proposal. I had once been to tea with him at his chambers in the quaint old Inn, and the idea of actually owning and living in those picturesque cosy rooms simply delighted me. The other women who "infested the place" – what a disgusting expression to use! – I could have done without, not being at all thin-skinned or conventional, but they wouldn't be in my way. And the idea of the night porter was delicious. I could stroll in, if I pleased, at three o'clock in the morning and there would be no one there to say: "My *goodness*, Phyllis! Where *have* you been?" Yes, Clifford's Inn would suit me to a capital T.

As soon as I arrived in London, I made a bee-line for the little passage by St Dunstan's church and introduced myself. Mr Larkin was a duck – if you can imagine a duck in a frock coat and a chimney-pot hat. For that was what he wore. He wasn't a bit like a porter. On the contrary, he was a reverend and fatherly person of quite a superior class and most kind and sympathetic. I suspect that he secretly disapproved of me, as another "infester," but he didn't show it. And when he introduced me to Charlie's "set" – number twenty-four, second pair – I found that he had not only had the rooms swept and garnished but had even laid in a little store of provisions. So I took the key from him gratefully and forthwith entered into residence as a full-blown bachelor girl.

The models' ball was to come off in about a week's time, and many an anxious hour I spent considering what costume I should wear. I went over all the usual characters: Queen Elizabeth, Pierrette, Cleopatra and so forth. But, besides being stale and hackneyed, they all offered the same very serious objection. They all required a special wig. But I was, as the schoolboys say, "fed up" with wigs. Besides, no one in England knew about my wig, and I didn't mean that they should until my hair had grown. So wig characters were off. As to going as a pillar-box or a milk-churn, that would never do, for the guests would be mostly artists and they would hoot any trash of that kind from the room.

It was by the merest chance that the difficulty was solved, and solved in a most startling manner. I happened to be clearing out Charlie's wardrobe to make room for my own things, and a pretty business it was, for Charles was a bit of a dandy and decidedly extravagant in the matter of clothes. Now, I had shaken out and refolded four suits when it suddenly occurred to me to try one on and see what sort of man I should have made. And a mighty surprise I got from the experiment, for as Charlie is a rather small man whereas I am decidedly tall though slight – what dressmakers call a "smart figure" – I expected that I should hardly be able to get into his clothes. Imagine my astonishment, then, when I found them not only an easy fit but actually rather long in – well, in the ankles. Evidently the standard of size is not the same in men as in women.

But when I looked into the glass, I got quite a shock. It was a long glass – the door of the wardrobe, in fact – and showed the whole figure; and the figure was simply that of a young man. I hadn't my wig on, of course; I didn't usually wear it indoors when I was alone, so there was absolutely no hint of anything feminine in the figure that looked out at me from the glass. But it wasn't that which gave me such a shock. What really staggered me was my extraordinary resemblance to Charlie. It was perfectly astounding.

I had always understood that Charlie and I were very alike (he was my father's sister's son), but this was a revelation. It wasn't mere likeness; the figure in the glass was Charlie himself.

I was still staring like a gaby at my reflection when the idea, the momentous idea, presented itself; being introduced to my mind, no doubt, by the unmentionable person who invents ideas of that kind. Of course you've guessed what it was. 'It was obvious enough. One of the suits that I had just turned out was a dress suit. Goodness knows how many of them that scallywag cousin of mine possessed. But here was one. Very well. Then I wouldn't go to the models' ball as Ashtoreth or Nell Gwynn or Joan of Arc; I would just go as Mr Charles Sidley in the ordinary evening dress of an English gentleman. And I would take care to get there early.

What a lark it would be! Imagine Charlie's astonishment when he turned up and found that he had arrived ten minutes after himself. And what a state of befoozlement the other fellows would be in. For there was my unfortunate deep voice which the Munich gentleman had objected to: it was exactly like Charlie's voice. If I only played my part properly they would be hard put to it to tell which of the two Dromios was the genuine article.

The more I thought over my precious scheme the more delighted I was with it, and I nearly laughed myself into hysterics over the various little extra turns of "business" that I proposed to introduce into my rendering of the character of Mr Charles Sidley. To my impatience it seemed as if the week would never end. But it did at last, and the fateful day arrived.

I began my preparations absurdly early and was fully figged out three-quarters of an hour before it was time to start. I had hunted out an opera hat of Charlie's – it was decidedly too big but was quite possible if you didn't jam it on too hard – and had got myself a suitable pair of shoes and gloves; and in these and a light overcoat of Charlie's and a muffler, I fidgeted about the room in an agony of fear lest somebody should come to the door and prevent me from escaping. At last, unable to bear the suspense any longer, I popped out, shut the door after me very quietly, and sneaked down the stairs in a frightful state of self-consciousness.

My misfortunes began on the first-floor landing. I was just turning the corner when a shadowy form arose from the next flight below, and developed into a coarse-looking man.

"Hallo!" said he; "here you are, then."

It sounded like a truism, but, of course, it wasn't. More to the point was his next remark.

"Caught yer on the 'op this time, I 'ave."

The vulgar familiarity of his tone was intolerable. I covered him with a haughty stare and demanded coldly: "And, pray, who might you be?"

His eyes opened until I felt quite nervous. They looked as if they really must drop right out.

"Oo might I be?" he repeated slowly. "Well, I might be the Lord Mayor or the Dook o' York. But I ain't."

"I didn't ask who you were not. The question is who you are?"

He stared at me silently for some seconds and then exclaimed with deep conviction: "Well, I'm jiggered."

"Are you, indeed?" said I. "But I don't think I remember anyone of that name."

This seemed to nettle him, for he advanced in a threatening manner and exclaimed: "Look 'ere, Mister Blooming Sidley, I don't want none of your sauce. I want my money, that's what I want. Gimme any more back answers and I'll set abaat yer."

I haven't the least idea what the creature meant; but at this moment the door of the first-floor set opened about three-quarters of an inch and an inquisitive eye appeared in the chink. It was really most uncomfortable.

"How much do you want?" I asked.

"Two pounds eleven and four-pence is what I want," he replied, with suspicious readiness, adding: "You ought to know the amount by this time, I should think."

Now, I had dropped some five or six pounds into my – or rather Charlie's – trousers pocket in case of emergencies, so I decided to pay this insolent wretch and get rid of him. Accordingly I handed him three pounds, and, having received the change, together with a greasy-looking receipt and a very surly "good evening," I waited on the landing for him to clear off and watched from the window his departure towards Fetter Lane. Then I followed – and the door on the landing closed softly.

I went out through the Fetter Lane gate myself to avoid passing the lodge and possibly encountering Mr Larkin. In Fleet Street I hailed a hansom and breathed more freely when once I was inside it and safe from any further chance meetings with embarrassing strangers. But that encounter with Charlie's creditor – his name was Jacob Blunt according to the receipt, which, however, gave no further particulars beyond "account rendered" – had produced a most pernicious effect; it had shattered my confidence at a blow and taken all the fizzle out of the adventure.

However, when we drew up at the hall where the dance was taking place, I pulled myself together, and, having hopped out of the cab and paid the driver, sprang up the stone steps, three at a time in the finest athletic style. Unfortunately, I missed a step near the top and came down on all fours; and my hat fell off and bounced all the way down the steps, so that I had to go back and fetch it; and the cabman, whom I had lavishly overpaid, actually laughed – laughed out quite loud, the vulgar, impertinent creature!

I was in rather a quandary as to which cloak-room I ought to leave my things in. Was I a lady or a gentleman? I really couldn't say under the peculiar circumstances, but, fortunately, as it turned out, I decided to leave my hat and coat among the others of their kind in the gentlemen's cloak-room.

The adventure fell flatter and flatter. In my anxiety to forestall Charlie, I had arrived much too soon, and, when I entered the great bare hall, less than a dozen people were there. All of them were strangers to me, and all but two were women. And not a fancy dress among them. Up in the refreshment gallery a man was cutting sandwiches and whistling, and the four members of the orchestra were reading newspapers. It was a dreary beginning. I hung about in corners watching the guests arrive in twos and threes and wishing that Charlie would come. Of course, as soon as he turned up the fun would begin; in fact, I ought to have arrived after him instead of before.

I was standing some half-way up the stairs that led to the gallery, leaning over the balustrade with a wistful eye on the entrance when someone behind me said, "Hal-lo!" and gave me a most awful spank with the open hand. I spun round, crimson with fury – for it hurt most abominably, to say nothing of the indignity – and confronted a round-faced massive young man who was regarding me with a genial grin. But the grin faded instantly when he saw my face.

"How dare you!" I spluttered, "you – you – "

"Oh, I'm awfully sorry," he exclaimed, "Mistook you for another man. Frightfully sorry, I am, indeed. Beastly sorry!"

"What's the use of being sorry?" I demanded fiercely. And what use was it? Poppy and camomile fomentations would have been more to the point.

"Now, Timothy White!" said a feminine voice, "don't be cross and give way to angry passions. He didn't mean any harm."

I looked round. The remark proceeded from a brazen creature in pea-green stockings – and other things, of course – who was coming down the stairs with a man.

"Excuse me," I replied stiffly; "my name is Sidley."

"Well, of course, we know that, Silly Billy," the girl rejoined. "But you're Timothy White, too, and very cross you look. Now, why don't you try to look pleasant as you usually do?"

"Yes, don't be a fool, Sidley," said her companion. "Let me introduce you to Chaffers."

With an uneasy suspicion that I had been making a donkey of myself, I held out my hand to Chaffers, who gave it a friendly squeeze that nearly reduced it to jelly and me to tears.

"That's better, Timothy," said Miss Green-stockings; "If you're a good boy I'll give you a dance presently. Come along, Bernardo; they're just going to begin."

To my intense relief the pair moved off. Evidently they were intimate friends of Charlie's, and, as I had not even gathered their names, I should have had to let the cat out of the bag if they had stayed.

"Rum girl, Becky," remarked Chaffers, apparently alluding to Green-stockings. "Good sort, though. Works hard, keeps her sister's kids. Sister's a widow, you know."

I didn't know, but I made some vaguely appropriate reply. And Chaffers and I stood looking over the balustrade, conversing jerkily and each anxious to get rid of the other.

"Hallo!" exclaimed Chaffers, "there's Barker. Know him? Chap I took you for. I'll go and spank him now," and away he went, leaving me to slink away to an obscure corner where I could watch the entrance.

A quarter of an hour passed, and still there was no sign of Charlie. And then came the catastrophe.

I was staring hopelessly downwards through the gathering crowd when I noticed the companion of Green-stockings looking about anxiously as if seeking someone.

Suddenly he caught my eye and approached quickly, followed by a man with flat feet and an alpaca jacket, evidently an attendant.

"I say, Sidley," said my unknown friend, "there's something in the wind. A man has been asking for you in the cloakroom, and Spooner says he looks like a plain-clothes bobby."

"He's a plain-clothes man right enough, sir," said Spooner. "I spotted him directly. You see, I've been in the Force myself."

My heart sank. I felt as if I were going to faint. The whole horror of the situation burst on me in a flash. Of course my explanations would be scouted. Who would believe that I was a woman, with my short hair? Alas! the make-up was fatally perfect. For better or worse – especially worse – I was Charles Sidley.

There was no escape from the borrowed identity. I should be haled off to prison and there would be a most hideous scandal. Oh! Why did I ever embark on this fool's enterprise?

"There's no need to upset yourself, old man," my friend said encouragingly. "We'll see you through. You just give me your cloak-room ticket and I'll get your hat and coat and put 'em on. Then I'll go out at the front and nip round into Mogle Street and meet you at the back entrance. Spooner will show you the way."

"It's most awfully good of you!" I exclaimed, ready to fall on his neck and weep. But he was perfectly stolid, taking my ticket without a word and slipping away through the crowd on his mission of mercy.

"This is the way, sir," said Spooner, opening a door and letting me through into a passage; and as we made our way to the back of the premises, he continued: " 'Tis lucky for you, sir, that I spotted that man waiting for you like a cat at a mouse-hole. He'd have had you to a certainty if I hadn't."

I expressed − sincerely enough, Heaven knows! − my heartfelt gratitude, and Mr Spooner conducted me down some stairs to a door, which he opened with a great show of caution. As he looked out, I noticed that he held his hand in a peculiar position as if he were trying whether it was raining, and I took the opportunity to drop a half-sovereign into it, on which the hand closed automatically.

"Here comes Mr 'Adley, sir," he said, as footsteps were heard approaching. "You'd best put on your coat inside there and then cross the road to the turning oppersight and make for the King's Road."

Here Hadley − my new and most dear friend − came running in, peeling off my overcoat, which he helped me to put on.

"The plain-clothes chappie looked rather hard at me," he said, as he clapped my hat on my head, "but I don't think he tumbled to anything. Still, you'd better look alive. There, that'll do, old chap," − for I had seized both his hands and could have hugged him − "don't waste time. You go up that street opposite and leg it like the devil. Bobby may have smelt a rat, you know. So long." He pushed me out on the pavement and I at once crossed the road and darted up the narrow street, not only following his advice to "leg it," but, as an extra precaution, shooting round the first corner that I came to, and thereafter turning up every side-street that I encountered. My progress was thus an elaborate zig-zag, like that of a fugitive hare, and, at the end of ten minutes I reckoned that I had so far placed myself beyond pursuit that I ventured to moderate my pace. In fact I should have been quite easy in my mind if I had only had the faintest idea where I was.

Unfortunately I had not. The only thing that was quite clear was that I had got into a very undesirable neighbourhood, and I was just considering the desirability of asking my way when I was startled by a series of shrieks. I hurried forward, and turning a corner, beheld a strange and terrible sight. In the middle of the road a man and a woman were gyrating madly. The man grasped the woman by the hair and pounded her with his free fist, and at each thump the woman screeched and clawed at the man's face. A few men and boys looked on unconcernedly from doorways and a number of women stood along the kerb and gave technical advice to the woman.

I was petrified with horror. Never before had I seen a man strike a woman. My blood boiled at the sight, and, totally forgetting my peculiar circumstances, I pushed through the crowd and strode up to the ruffian.

"Let that poor woman go, you brute!" I exclaimed fiercely.

He did not let go but he stopped punching to stare at me.

"Do you hear me?" I demanded. "How dare you strike a woman, you miserable, cowardly wretch?"

He let go then, and the liberated woman ran towards me, for protection, as I supposed. But no such thing, for the first news that I had of her arrival was a bang at the crown of my hat that drove it down over my eyes like an extinguisher. Frantically I wrenched it off just in time to see the man advancing on me with the action of a dancing bear and flourishing a pair of the dirtiest and most enormous fists that I have ever seen. I backed away hurriedly – on to the woman, who immediately grabbed my collar and pulled it over my ear; and as I wriggled myself free, that horrid ruffian struck me a most fearful blow just under my left arm.

I gave a scream of agony – at which the women laughed joyously – and sprang back. Then the woman came at me with her fingers hooked like talons and the man advanced once more in the dancing bear style. It was an awful moment. I gazed in terror from one assailant to the other, and then – I turned and flew down the street like an antelope. A yell of mingled laughter and execration arose behind me, but I heeded it not. A female voice – that of the rescued woman, I fear – bawled "Yah! Cow – WURD!" But I didn't care. I had no false pride. The vital necessity was to put as great a distance as possible between me and those terrible fists.

At first I had a small attendant procession of boys and men, but they soon dropped behind. Either I outdistanced them or they went back to witness the sequel. But I still ran on, up one street and down another, until I reached a quieter neighbourhood, and here I paused to get my breath and wipe my eyes – not that I was crying, you know, only that awful thump had made my eyes run a little.

I had tucked in my collar as well as I could and attended to my hat – of which one of the springs had gone wrong, causing it to develop a most singular hump on one side – when I came out into a wider street at the corner of which stood two policemen, a sergeant and a constable. The sergeant stepped forward briskly when he saw me.

"Anything the matter, sir?" he asked in a suspicious tone.

"Yes," I answered. "A horrid wretch of a man has been knocking a woman about most dreadfully."

"Whereabouts was this?" asked the sergeant.

"Well, I really don't quite know. Somewhere in that direction," I said, pointing vaguely up the street.

"Hope you didn't interfere, sir," said the sergeant, with a sly leer at his subordinate.

I had to admit that I did and, moreover, to describe the disastrous consequences.

"Punched you in the ribs, did he?" said the sergeant. "And what did you do?"

"I ran away as fast as I could."

"Did you though," said the sergeant.

"J'ear that, Moloney?"

"Oi did," replied the constable, "an' 'twas the best thing too. Ye did quite right, sir, only ye began at the wrong end."

"What do you mean?" I demanded.

"Whoy, ye began with valour and ye ended with discretion. Now I'd try the discretion first next time if I was you." And here the two policemen actually laughed in my face.

I turned away, very red and angry. Policemen are generally so polite to me, too. But I suppose it was that bulging hat and the torn collar. At any rate I stalked away down the street and was just turning the corner when I chanced to look back. A tall man was talking to the policemen, and, as I looked back, both officers pointed in my direction. Then the man began to run – towards me; and then the policemen began to run, too.

A thrill of terror shot through me. I saw it all in a flash of intuition. It was the plain-clothes man. He had traced me from the hall and was now close on my heels. I gave a last despairing glance and once more sped away on the wings of the wind.

I don't know how those great clumsy wretches did it, but they not only kept me in sight; they actually gained on me. I ran on with dwindling hope and failing breath until suddenly, far up the street, I saw something that heartened me for a final spurt. It was a taxicab, drawn up by the kerb. The chauffeur saw at a glance how things were, and beckoned wildly. Then he wound up his machine with the fury of an insane organ-grinder, opened the door, sprang to his seat and turned the cab half round. One more burst and I was free.

Then came an unexpected check. A little crowd of women in brightly coloured hats – all alike – came out of some kind of public hall and watched my approach.

"Stop that man," yelled one of the policemen, whereupon a small, bumptious looking woman ran into the road and sang out: "All right, policeman. I'll stop him."

As I drew near she stretched out her arms as if I had been a runaway cow. I suppose she thought I should have to stop to avoid hurting her.

But she was mistaken. My ribs still ached from the thump that I had received. But I had not been thumped in vain. I had learned something. So did she when I drove my knuckles into her armpit and upset her in the gutter. Of course her colleagues raised a howl – so did she, for that matter – of "brute," "coward," and so forth. But they kept out of reach.

"Look alive, sir!" bawled the chauffeur. I must have looked extremely alive already but I put on a final spurt and at last dived into the open cab. As I slammed the door, something went "bang! whirr!" The cab started with a jerk; the horn sang "honk! honk!" and the engine played an ascending chromatic scale as it picked up speed.

The night porter looked at me a little queerly as he let me in. Perhaps it was only my misshapen hat and imperfectly adjusted collar. But whatever it was, I breathed more freely when I was safely bolted in Charlie's chambers. I undressed like lightning and packed that wretched suit out of sight; and even then I left a glimmer of gas on all night and kept my wig ready to clap on at a moment's notice.

FLIGHT TWO

The Minotaur

If I were asked to name the outstanding characteristic of my sex I should say it is persistency. It has been said that a woman does not know when she is beaten. But this is untrue. She does, and so does everybody else in the neighbourhood. Only the knowledge doesn't influence her conduct. Of which truth the present history furnishes a case in point.

Any person who has read of my last adventure would suppose that I should have had enough of masquerading in male attire. I thought so myself at first. But it was a mistake. I had tasted of the joys of masculinity and I secretly hankered to taste again – with a little less seasoning, perhaps. But I don't suppose I ever should, had not circumstance once more stepped in and given me the necessary push off.

I had now taken over my cousin Charlie's chambers at 24 Clifford's Inn. On the jamb of the entry "Mr C Sidley" had been painted out and "Miss Dudley" had been painted in. But Charlie's furniture remained in the rooms and so did a considerable quantity of his clothes, to my great inconvenience. And there they were likely to remain for the present; for Charlie had been doing something naughty and was now living in strict retirement – lying low in fact. Which was a contributory circumstance to my next escapade. But there was another and a more important one.

My little flat was perfectly delightful but for one defect. In the bedroom ceiling, right over the bed, was a trap-door; and not a wooden trap, but a mere frame filled in with perforated zinc. Of course, anyone in the loft – into which it opened – could look down into my bedroom. It was most uncomfortable. But this wasn't the worst. One day it occurred to me to see if it was perfectly secure, and, stepping up on the bed – for the ceiling was quite low – I gave it a push with my hand. Imagine my horror when the trap immediately went up without the slightest resistance! There was no fastening whatever.

Here was a nice state of affairs! I stared up in dismay at the yawning square hole; all my security was gone. Of what use was it to bolt the oaken outer door at night, with an unguarded trap opening into my very sanctum? But, of course, the loft was kept locked and the key in the porter's lodge. There wasn't really any danger – provided there were no other traps.

In an instant, I had lifted an empty trunk on to the bed and mounted on it with my head through the opening. Grasping the side of the hole – I am a pretty athletic young person – and giving a spring, I shot up like a harlequin and pulled myself fairly through until I knelt on the floor of the loft. I stood up and looked about me. It was a great ruinous-looking place and quite dark, save for the glimmer that oozed in between the tiles and through the cracks of the closed shutters that guarded the unglazed dormer. The rubbish of centuries lay piled around, the shapeless heaps looming obscurely through the dim twilight, but in the middle there was a considerable space of clear floor. I glanced down through the hole, on the bed on which I had slept with so much unjustified confidence, and then began to walk along the floor; and I had not walked a dozen paces when there appeared at my feet another square space through which a dim light filtered. There was another trap, then.

I knelt down beside the opening with my ear close to the perforated zinc and listened intently. No sound came up from the chambers. Then I grasped the frame of the trap and gave a pull;

and, sure enough, up it came. There was no fastening here, either. A pretty state of things for an unprotected girl! My little flat was in absolute communication with another, and who could say what sort of ruffian the tenant of that other flat might be?

I looked down on a patch of bare floor beneath, and then, with some compunction, I ventured to thrust my head through the opening. But I looked into an empty room. And on this, I suddenly remembered, with a thrill of relief, that the second-floor "set" in the building next to mine was empty and to let. So, for the present, I could feel that my little castle was safe from intrusion, provided there were no more traps opening into the loft. And there were not. I satisfied myself very thoroughly on that point by a careful exploration of the loft – which, in fact, covered only these two sets of chambers; and so, having set my mind at rest on this momentous question, I dropped down, with a good deal more agility than dignity, into my own bedroom and closed the trap.

I thought a good deal about that passage-way through into the next house, and I dare say I should have thought a good deal more if I had only known what an extraordinary part it was to play – but, there! I mustn't begin moralizing in advance; I didn't know; and perhaps I should have acted in just the same way if I had.

The spark that, so to speak, exploded the mine was a middle-aged spark. He was coming out of the Hotel Cecil when I first saw him, and for one moment, I caught his eye. Then I looked away, for it was a bad eye, dark, glittering, hypnotic; and it had lighted up with a sudden, intent admiration that made me feel horrid. I like admiration as much as any girl, but not that kind, thank you. Besides, he was old enough to be my father.

I walked on quickly, just a little annoyed. That single glance had left me with a vivid impression of a sleek, over-dressed, wealthy-looking man of near upon fifty; dark, rather handsome and evidently not English. Of course, the English nation does not contain all the good people in the world; but still – well he looked like a foreigner, at any rate, and you must remember that I have travelled and lived on the Continent.

At Charing Cross I turned into the National Gallery (having forgotten all about the obnoxious stranger) and proceeded to call upon the old favourites that I had been used to study when I was working at the Slade School. My first visit was to Cornelius Van der Geest, whose portrait I had once copied – a shockingly bad copy it was, too – and I was standing gazing at the long, melancholy face and wondering what Master Van Dyk would think of our modern "progressive art" – Matisse or Van Gogh, for instance – when I became aware of someone standing behind me, looking over my shoulder. After a minute or so, I moved away from the picture, and, happening to glance back. was a good deal startled at recognizing the foreign person of the Hotel Cecil. To be sure, he had as much right there as I, but – well, I trotted off in mighty quick time, and, crossing the building, made for the new room where the Corots hang. Here, in front of Israel's great picture, I was inspecting my reflection in the glass – which is about all that you can see – when that reflection was unostentatiously joined by another. I didn't have to look round this time, with that great Claude Lorraine mirror before me; I could see the newcomer's figure quite plainly, and once more I moved off.

The sort of infatuation that impels an elderly man to pursue a mere girl is a complete mystery to me. This foreign wretch must have seen that I hated him, but yet he kept at my heels until I had led him through every room in the place. By this time my annoyance was beginning to give way to amusement. It was really getting quite farcical; and as we had now exhausted the galleries, I decided to take my follower for a walk outside and show him the town. It wasn't very discreet but it was quite entertaining. I trotted him up and down Oxford Street, I showed him Regent Street and Piccadilly, I let him see the last word in hats and costumes and introduced him to all the principal jewellers and picture shops. It was an absurd affair and very silly of me; but I thought it a great joke at the time, and goodness knows how long I should have gone on enjoying "the pleasures of the chase," as Eugene Wrayburn has it, if I had not suddenly grown tired and wishful to get home and make myself a cup of tea. Then, of course, arose the necessity of shaking off my pursuer, for it would never do to let him know where I lived; and this I thought I had managed rather neatly, for, having worked my way to Fleet Street, I darted ahead, shot up Clifford's Inn Passage and scuttled into my burrow like an alarmed rabbit.

I saw no more of my foreign friend, but a couple of days later a very queer thing happened. I had taken off my wig and was examining my short hair in the glass, wondering how soon it would have grown to a manageable length, when there came a hurried tapping at my outer door. I was just about to clap on my wig and go out to open it when a thought made me pause. One has to be careful when one lives alone in a flat.

Now the provident Charlie had devised a very neat little spy-hole by which one could peep out and see who was on the landing. Slipping off my shoes, I tiptoed into the sitting-room and applied my eye to the spy-hole. Then I saw that my visitor was a woman; and something in her appearance decided me to leave the door unopened.

She continued to knock, softly but urgently. Apparently she knew that I was in. But still I made no move. Then she addressed me through the letter-slit, with a slight foreign accent.

"Please open the door, Miss. It is very important," and, as I disregarded this request, too, she continued: "It is very urgent. You shall see when you read the letter"; and here a note was slipped through and fell to the bottom of the open letter-box. At the risk of being seen, I picked it out and stole through to the bedroom to read it, and this was what it said:

"Dear Madam. – An old woman who lies dying in our house wishes to see you. She will not tell us her true name but she says that she has an important secret which she can only tell to Miss Dudley of Clifford's Inn. So please come with bearer who will show you the house.

Yours truly,

Mrs Stokes.

"P.S. – The secret relates to a hidden will and a very great property."

Of course, that settled it. I wasn't born yesterday. "Bogus" was writ large all over this precious document. Besides, no one but Charlie knew that I was living in Clifford's Inn. But it was very mysterious. It looked like some sort of trap. And then I had a sudden inspiration. I would follow this good lady and give her address and the note to the police. It was an excellent idea and ought to have come off triumphantly if I hadn't carried it out like an arrant booby.

The knocking still went on; and meanwhile I whisked off my clothes like lightning and hustled myself into a plain tweed suit of Charlie's, but putting on my own stout walking shoes. I dropped some loose money and my latch-key into my pocket, clapped on one of Charlie's hats, snatched up my walking stick, and, lifting a trunk on the bed, stepped on it and pushed up the trap-door. In a moment I had scrambled up into the loft, and, stepping lightly along to the next trap, lifted it and looked down. The ceiling was barely eight feet from the floor, but it looked a long way; however, I boldly slipped through the opening and let myself down until I hung by my fingers, when I let go and dropped lightly on the bare boards.

After a glance through the dusty windows to make sure that the porter was not about, I walked through the empty rooms, and, letting myself out quietly, ran down the stairs. All was well so far. But now, yielding to an impulse of mere mischief, I did a most supremely idiotic thing. Strolling round the building, I walked straight into my own entry and began to ascend the stairs. Half-way up, I met a thick-set, seedy-looking man, who, as he passed me, gave a quick stare and then looked away.

I took the last flight as quietly as possible and surprised the woman in the act of listening at my letter-box. She looked rather startled at my sudden appearance and stepped back to make way for me. I went through the form of rapping at the "oak" with the handle of my stick and then, after waiting a few moments, turned to the woman – who now looked more startled than ever – and remarked: "There doesn't appear to be anyone at home."

"No, it seems not," she replied, settling herself by the recess of the landing window and running an attentive eye over my person. I didn't much enjoy her scrutiny, especially when it seemed to focus itself on my shoes, so I turned and retreated down the stairs, where, oddly enough, I met the same man coming up with a notebook in his hand. Again he looked at me inquisitively, but I ran past him, and, emerging into the square, took up a position in a deep doorway whence I could watch the entry to my staircase. In about a minute the woman came out, and, without looking round, walked across the square and out through the back gate into Fetter Lane.

Now came the pleasures of the chase indeed! Out into the Lane, down Fleet Street, over Blackfriars Bridge, I followed that unconscious woman with the greatest ease, for the crowd screened me and she never looked back. I had no idea that shadowing was so easy. But once over the bridge it became less simple, for the woman turned down a side street that led into a waterside neighbourhood, and here, as there were fewer people about, I had to keep a greater distance. It was not a nice district and the inhabitants were not of a pleasing type, but I stuck doggedly to my quarry until she suddenly turned and disappeared through the arched entrance to a narrow alley. I stepped forward quickly, but by the time I reached the entrance to the alley, the woman had disappeared. I halted, gazing irresolutely up the squalid little court, debating whether I should pursue my investigations any farther, when the question was decided for me. Some invisible person, who had approached noiselessly from behind, suddenly grasped me by the arms and ran me through the narrow archway, up the dark entry and into an open door, which, however, immediately became a closed door.

Recovering somewhat from my astonishment, I began to wriggle violently and would have shouted but that a dirty hand was clapped over my mouth and gave me abundant reason for keeping it shut. At the same moment the foreign woman emerged from the gloom and took possession of my wrists.

"It's of no use for you to struggle and make a noise, young woman," she remarked; "you're not going to be hurt as long as you keep quiet."

"Young woman!" exclaimed a husky voice from the darkness behind the previous speaker, "why, it's a man!"

"Is it?" said the woman, scornfully.

"You look at that pretty little emerald ring on 'er finger" – here she lifted up my right hand for inspection – "d'ye ever see a man wear a ring like that? I twigged it when I see 'er knockin' at 'er own door. And look at them shoes and open-work stockings. No, she's been a bit too artful this time, she 'as"; which was undoubtedly the fact.

Here a powerful and most repulsive-looking ruffian appeared from the inner darkness, and, gripping my wrists, looked closely at my hands, particularly at the dainty little emerald ring.

"Take yer paw off 'er mug, Joe, and let's 'ave a look at 'er," said he, adding reassuringly, "I'll bash 'er if she 'ollers."

The paw was accordingly withdrawn and I was pushed roughly against the wall that my captors might inspect me; and now, in spite of the dim light, I was able to recognize in the owner of the paw the man whom I had met on my staircase.

Terrified as I naturally was, my mind worked rapidly as I stood pinned against that grimy wall. If I could only get to the door – but I couldn't, for the wretch, Joe, was between it and me, and the flight of stairs that I could dimly see at the other end of the passage only seemed to lead farther from safety. Meanwhile the three wretches calmly discussed where they should put me and finally decided, to my unspeakable horror, that I should be safest in the cellar. To this secluded retreat they were apparently about to remove me when I felt the grip on my wrists relax somewhat. With an instantaneous jerk I twisted myself free and darted off in the only possible direction, towards the stairs. Of course, they were after me in a moment, the woman leading, but it was a narrow staircase and they could only come up in single file. Near the top of the first flight I halted suddenly and kicked out like a donkey. My foot encountered something soft, the woman gave a loud yell and immediately there followed a sound as of an avalanche of Saratoga trunks. I didn't stop to see what had happened, but ran up and darted into the first room that I came to. There was not much furniture in it, but there was a small table, and when I had shut the door and jammed this table upside down and slanting under the knob, it answered the purpose as well as one of Chubbs' safe locks. No one could possibly get in. The only question was whether anyone could get out.

I will do my friends the justice to say that they were not easily discouraged. The place shook as if from the combined effects of an earthquake, a volcanic eruption and a modern American dance. And there were verbal accompaniments too, which I heard but imperfectly and understood not at all. But the hubbub served its purpose, for it enabled me, unnoticed, to open the window and survey the prospect; which was neither lovely nor inspiriting, consisting of a paved yard, a wooden fence, the back of a sort of factory building and, immediately beneath me, a sloping slate roof.

In an instant my resolution was taken. The door was audibly cracking behind me. In a few moments my pursuers would be at my heels. Grasping the window sill, I swung myself out and immediately went slithering down the slates until I came to the eaves, when I dropped, all of a heap, with a most awful thump, on the pavement beneath. Almost at the same moment, a hideous crash above told me that the door had at last given way.

I picked myself up as quickly as I could and cast a terrified look around. The little yard into which I had fallen had but one exit, which was the back door of the house. Realizing that there was no escape for me that way, I made a dash at the fence and was frantically endeavouring to scramble up it when the whole pack of miscreants came rushing out of the back door. In a moment the two men had seized me and were trying to drag me away while I clung to the fence and cried out lustily for help. Just as I was torn from my hold and was being hustled back towards the house, a man appeared at the open window of the factory building that overlooked the yard. For one moment he stared at us in sheer amazement; then climbing out, he let himself down from the sill and dropped into the yard.

The appearance of that man altered the situation completely. He was a biggish man, very squarely built, and he seemed to know his own mind, for he came across the yard like a short-horn bull and without a word fell to hammering the two men, incidently sitting the woman on the pavement with a dexterous twist of his elbow. I had never seen anything like that man's quickness. You could hardly see his fists though no doubt you could feel them, and he was as expert with his feet as a cathedral organist. Man has been said to be a cooking animal. This man appeared to be a fighting animal, and I, who like most women, am a somewhat bumptious animal, felt a new-born respect for his sex.

But it was all very confusing. I was quite bewildered for the moment. The men gyrated wildly round one another like fighting-cocks. The woman screeched and tried to scramble up until one of her confederates tripped and sat on her stomach, and then she screeched louder. My wits returned somewhat suddenly when this man sprang up with a broad, wicked-looking knife in his hand and tried to get behind my champion. In a moment I had fastened with both hands on his wrist and held on regardless of the thumps that he delivered with the other hand. My warrior soon came to my assistance, having knocked out the other man, and together we pinned the knifebearer against the wall, where the warrior endeavoured to disarm him while I kept off the woman with occasional demonstrations with my foot. Meanwhile the defeated ruffian – it was the one called Joe – darted into the house and, in a few seconds, rushed out again holding a large and very odd-looking pistol. There was no time to think. I simply rushed at him like an infuriated cat and grabbed him as best I could. What followed is a mere whirl of confusion. The man staggered backwards, the pistol began to go off with a rapid succession of reports that I thought would never cease, the other ruffian uttered a loud cry, the woman screeched, and then the warrior rushed at us and felled my assailant with a terrific blow on the jaw. And then in a moment the affair was over. The villain Joe lay unconscious on the pavement, the other ruffian was a huddled heap by the wall, and the woman, scared out of her senses, stood whimpering and looking from one to the other.

There was a moment's pause: a moment of chilly reaction; then there arose on the air the thin, high note of a police whistle, followed by a loud banging at the street door.

My champion gave me a quick glance. "Look here, Sidley," said he, "you don't want any truck with the bobbies, do you?"

I certainly did not, and said so.

"Then we'd better clear out before they break in," said he. "Let me give you a hoist over the fence."

It didn't occur to me to ask how he going to get over. Unconsciously I assumed that he could do anything he pleased, and I accepted his help without a word. He grasped me quickly below the knees and gave a vigorous hoist while I clutched at the top of the fence, and before I knew what was happening, I found myself on my back, on a heap of ashes, looking up at a masterful figure that straddled over the top rail.

"Now, old chap," said he as he sprang lightly down, "we'd better leg it." And leg it we did across some unutterably filthy patches of waste ground, through the purlieus of several wharves and finally out into some sort of goods-yard or siding, where a number of railway trucks stood about disconsolately. Here we stopped for a few moments to listen, and to my unutterable horror, the shrill notes of a police whistle arose quite near at hand.

"By Jove!" exclaimed my champion, "we oughtn't to have bolted, but as we have, we'd better clear right away. Look out, Sidley!"

A file of empty trucks was coming down the line on which we were standing and threatened to nip us against two stationary waggons. As we sprang clear, my friend looked quickly at these latter.

"This'll do, Sidley," said he, "up you go!" and seizing me unceremoniously, he hoisted me up and bundled me over the side of the waggon, scrambling up after me as I rolled over on the unsavoury floor. "Now," he exclaimed, "stand by for the bump!" and he had hardly spoken when the approaching train struck our chariot with a crash that seemed to dislocate every joint in my body.

"Keep lying down flat," my companion whispered – most unnecessarily, for, after that jolt, I couldn't have got up for a thousand pounds. But there were no more upheavals at the moment, and, to my infinite relief, our conveyance continued to rumble on with no incident but the welcome clank as some pointsman hooked on the coupling. I don't know how far we travelled in that wretched, clattering conveyance, or how long it took us to cover the distance, for I was half insensible from the shock of the collision; but my next recollection is of the thing having stopped and of my being hauled out on to the line.

"Pull yourself together, Sidley," said my friend, giving me a slight shake-up; and I tried to collect my scattered wits as an official-looking person bore down on us with a threatening air.

"What might you two gentlemen want here?" the latter inquired a little stiffly, to which my friend replied: "We want to find the way out of this confounded place."

"You haven't got no business here at all," said the official, and having fired this shot, he conducted us through a sort of Hampton Court Maze of sheds and railway lines and finally delivered us into a narrow alley.

"We'd better get out of this neighbourhood as quickly as we can, Sidley," said my friend, setting me an excellent example in the matter of pace; and as we threaded our way through a seemingly endless succession of narrow streets, I found myself for the first time realizing with astonishment that I was being mistaken for my cousin Charlie. However, this was no time for explanations. My rescuer's walking powers were almost equal to his capacity for fighting, and it was all that I could do to make a decent show of trying to keep up with him.

We came to the surface, so to speak, at the foot of Vauxhall Bridge, by which time the daylight was beginning to fade. We walked at a more leisurely pace across the bridge and for the first time I had a chance of getting a good look at my companion. He was a fine-looking man, rather big and very powerful, as I have said, with a handsome, alert, and resolute face. I may as well admit that I liked the look of him amazingly, and especially I liked his eyes, which were of an unusual dark blue with something thoughtful and almost dreamy in them, which was queerly out of character with his late proceedings. And having noted these particulars, I thought that the time for explanations had come and proceeded to offer them.

"You have addressed me once or twice as Sidley," I said somewhat diffidently, "that isn't my name."

"The deuce it isn't!" he exclaimed, halting to look at me with such intentness that I felt myself turning scarlet.

"No." I stammered, "but I have a cousin named Charles Sidley, and we're very much alike. Perhaps you know him."

My new friend slapped his thigh. "By Jove!" he exclaimed, "I thought there was something queer, and I have been wondering all along what change could have come over Charlie. You're younger, aren't you?"

Now I really was about a fortnight younger than Charlie so I was able to say "yes" with a clear conscience, and then my friend asked suddenly: "By the way, what is your name?"

The question took me aback completely. What on earth was my name? I floundered guiltily for a few moments and then, inspired, I believe, by a combination of Phyllis and rowdy, I blurted out "My name is Philip Rowden."

My friend held out a cordial hand.

"Glad to know you, Rowden," said he, with a grip that made me wink. "You're a plucky young beggar and I like you. If you hadn't had some backbone, we should both have been either knifed or potted."

"It's very good of you to say so," I faltered, turning, I suspect, exceedingly pink, but he responded brusquely: "Stuff, my dear fellow, I don't pay compliments. Come and look me up one evening. I haven't many friends but I value those I have. This is where I live," and he presented me with a card on which I read: "Mr Paul Everard, 63, Jacob Street, Hampstead Road."

I took the card from him with some confusion, and I think he was rather surprised that I did not offer mine in exchange. But he made no remark, and we travelled together silently on an omnibus as far as Charing Cross. Here we both got down and he shook my hand once more until my ears tingled.

"Goodbye, old chap," he said cordially.

"Mind you look me up soon." I promised him I would, though of course I had no intention of doing any such thing.

Nevertheless, I don't mind admitting that when I got back to my chambers I changed into my very prettiest frock, and having carefully adjusted my wig, looked long and thoughtfully at myself in the glass, wondering whether Mr Paul Everard would not think me rather a nice-looking girl.

FLIGHT THREE

Mr Shylock

In the account of my first adventure I took the occasion to remark that I had been the victim of circumstances. And so I had. Not a very unwilling victim perhaps, but we won't go into that. I merely desire to point out that the responsibility for what happened rests upon circumstances and not upon me. Another profound observation that I venture to make is that the consequences of our actions seem to accumulate at a sort of compound interest; and having made these liberal contributions to the treasury of human wisdom, I shall proceed to illustrate them by a case in point.

First, I will remind you of my peculiar position. I had taken over my cousin Charlie's chambers in Clifford's Inn, a nice little flat on the top floor. In the next house on the same floor was a precisely similar set of chambers. Above those two flats was a disused loft. There was that trap-door which opened through the ceiling of my bedroom, and the similar trap in the bedroom ceiling of the next flat; neither trap having any fastening whatever. Of course it would be very convenient in case of fire; for I could pop up through my trap, run along the loft and drop down the other trap, and there I should be.

But supposing the occupant of the other flat came popping through into mine? That was quite a different pair of shoes. At present there wasn't any occupant, for that set of chambers was vacant. But it might let at any moment, and it was nearly certain to let to a man. Clearly the position was an impossible one. Perhaps you'll ask why I didn't adopt the obvious plan of having a bolt fixed to my trap. Well, I'll tell you. Because I didn't. So there!

Then there was my rescuer, Mr Paul Everard. In his innocence he actually believed me to be a young man – which shows what gabies men are. I should like to see any girl passing herself off on *me* as a man! Well, Paul – Mr Everard – had asked me to call on him, which I should have been delighted to do – for I had taken a decided fancy to him. But of course it wasn't to be thought of.

Nevertheless, I had a presentiment that I should meet Mr Everard again, and when a girl has a presentiment of that kind with regard to a man whom she is rather taken with, she is generally right. Because, you see, it is possible to give presentiments a little assistance.

But if I did happen to meet him, and chanced to be in male attire at the time – for otherwise he wouldn't recognize me – and if he asked, as he certainly would, where I lived, I should have to give him some address, and I obviously couldn't give him 24, Clifford's Inn, for that was the address of Miss Phyllis Dudley.

You see whither circumstances were leading. There was really only one perfectly reasonable and discreet thing to do, namely, to engage that next-door flat in the name of Mr Philip Rowden. By doing that I should settle the difficulty about those trap-doors, and if I ever again had a fancy to go abroad in masculine garments I should give to my masculine double "a local habitation and a name." But I didn't act precipitately. In fact, it is possible that I shouldn't have acted at all but that circumstance again stepped in – in a voluminous overcoat with the collar turned up and a wide-brimmed hat pulled down over his face.

Of course it was that scallywag, Charlie. He arrived at my flat at about nine in the evening, and, when I had opened the door, he slipped in quickly and closed it after him.

"My dear Charlie!" I exclaimed, "I had no idea you were in London – there, that will do; we aren't so affectionate as all that."

"I am," said Charlie.

"Well, I'm not," I retorted. "Handshaking is good enough for me. But I thought you were – well, I don't quite know where."

"Then you hit off my whereabouts to a 't' Phyl," said he with a grin, "and I may say that I shall be remaining in the same locality for some little time."

"I'm afraid you've been doing something naughty," I said in a reproving tone. "I heard something about a plain-clothes policeman who was looking for you."

"Oh, that's all right," he replied airily. "I've settled that. There was a slight misunderstanding. But I want you to help me in another little affair."

"Oh, do you?" I said, rather dryly.

"Yes. I'm in a bit of a corner about a bill."

"Tailor's bill?" I asked.

"No, not that sort of bill. Moneylender's bill – promise to pay, you know. It isn't my bill, but I backed it, and as the chappie who drew it can't pay at the moment, they'll drop on me; and as I can't meet it, why the fat'll be in the fire."

"You *are* an ass, Charlie!" I exclaimed.

"I know," he replied. "It runs in the family."

"Not on my side, thank you. But I suppose you want me to let you have some money?"

"Certainly not!" he replied indignantly. "Think I'd sponge on a girl? No, Phyl; just want you to leave a note for me and collect a walking-stick that I left at a house."

This sounded innocent enough, but the expression on Charlie's face as he made the proposal was so excessively leery that I smelt a rat at once.

"Charlie," I said, "you are up to some bedevilment. Now, own up or I won't move a finger to help you."

He sniggered guiltily but looked mighty pleased with himself all the same.

"All right, Phyl," said he. "I'll tell you all about it. And, in the first place, let me assure you that Mr Shylock is going to be paid either by me or the other chappie. Whichever of us gets the money first will pay up, and if Shylock would only give us a little time, there would be no trouble. But for private reasons of his own he won't give us a moment's grace. Well now, Mr S has a nice little house near Regent's Park and a nice little branch office at Brighton, which he visits three times a week. This bill was drawn at Brighton and is now in the office safe there. But Mr S resides at his London house. Do you see my drift?"

"Not in the least," I answered.

"Well, you see, I happen to be able to lay my hand on that bill – never mind how – "

"But you don't propose to steal it!" I exclaimed.

"Certainly not. Just to take care of it until my friend or I can meet it."

"And what do you want me to do?"

"Just what I said. You'll call at Shylock's house on Tuesday night at eight o'clock exactly and hand in the note and this umbrella, which I borrowed from Shylock some time ago, and ask the servant for the stick that I left in place of it. You'll say that you want the stick at once because I am just leaving town and you are going to see me off. The servant will give you the stick and will report what you said when she gives the note to Shylock and Mr S will have the information that I was in town at eight o'clock. Whereas, at that psychological moment I shall be hooking the bill out of his safe at Brighton, and, as I shall be careful to leave the office door ajar for the bobby to find on his next round, and thus fix the time, it will be quite a neat little alibi."

"But, my dear boy!" I exclaimed, "you are actually proposing to commit a burglary!"

"Oh, that's all right," he replied carelessly. "Nothing's going to be stolen and there'll be no risk. No use being frightened by mere technicalities."

All the same I *was* frightened; very, frightened indeed; and at first I refused to be implicated in the affair at all. But when he assured me that he intended to "collect the bill" (that was how he expressed it) whether I helped him or not, what could I do? I couldn't leave the poor, silly boy in the lurch. So, in the end, I took charge of the note and the umbrella and promised to deliver them both at the time stated to the handmaiden of Mr Moses McDougal.

But when I came to think over Charlie's scheme in cold blood, I didn't like it a bit. It was all very well to talk about technicalities, but breaking into an office and opening a safe is burglary and nothing else. And then, as to this alibi, as Charlie called it, it really was no alibi at all. There would be nothing but my bare statement to show that Charlie was in London, and our worthy friend, Shylock, was presumably not absolutely fresh from the incubator. He was not likely to be much influenced by a mere statement.

Of course you see whither these profound cogitations were necessarily leading; and you see the brilliant opportunity that circumstance was dangling before my nose. I had only to dress up in one of Charlie's suits and instead of leaving the note just to call and ask for my stick, leaving a verbal message for Shylock and there was an alibi that would lay out Mr Shylock as flat as a starfish.

Of course the mere carping critic will say that I could have carried out this little plan without engaging that next-door flat. Perhaps I could. It's easy to be wise after the event, but at the time it seemed to me that the possession of that second set of chambers was an indispensable part of the scheme, and, before there had been time for me to revise my opinion on the subject, I found myself pulling the bell at the Head Porter's lodge.

I almost blush when I recall the torrent of untruths that I poured into the ear of the unsuspecting Mr Larkin; but not quite, for it was circumstance and not I who wove that tissue of falsehood. Mr Larkin was quite interested to hear of my cousin, Mr Philip Rowden, and expressed the hope that he would be more punctual in paying his rent than my other cousin, Mr Charles Sidley, had been. This gave me just the opening that I wanted, for it enabled me to offer magnanimously to protect the landlord's interests by becoming the actual tenant myself with the right to sublet to my cousin Philip. To this proposal Mr Larkin agreed joyfully, and while he was having the agreement drawn, I went out and ordered a little suite of furniture – including a library ladder – and engaged a sign-writer to paint Mr Philip Rowden's name on the entry and above the door of the chambers. And if the connection between these activities and Charlie's escapade is still not obvious, I will give one further clue.

On taking off my wig and examining myself before the dressing glass, I found that my hair was getting quite long, which ought to have been quite a gratifying circumstance. Whether it was so, you may judge when I tell you that I forthwith changed into a suit of Charlie's and went out to look for a barber's shop, and I assure you that when I found myself seated in the chair, with a sort of extemporized surplice tucked in round my neck and the barber asked me if I would like a shave, I felt as proud as a pea-hen that has had its tail-feathers pulled out to ornament a screen.

By Tuesday evening, all the arrangements were completed. The agreement was signed, the name had been painted up, and a set of visiting-cards, bearing the name and address of Mr Philip Rowden, duly packed in a neat Russia leather case. Unfortunately, the furniture was not to be delivered until the following day, so that the latch-key was but a barren glory, and I had to start, as on previous occasions, from my own chambers.

It had barely turned six on that eventful evening when I took off my wig, and, having carefully parted and brushed my closely-cropped hair, began to change into one of Charlie's smart lounge suits. By half-past six the metamorphosis was complete, and, taking the precaution to put both latch-keys and a sufficiency of change in my pockets, I took Mr Shylock's umbrella from the corner, let myself out quietly, ran down the stairs and slipped unobtrusively out into Fetter Lane.

I don't mind admitting that I found something very exhilarating in walking through the streets in my borrowed plumage. It seemed to me that not only was I presenting a different exterior to the world, but that the world also presented a different exterior to me. Especially interested was I to observe with what singular unconcern the men whom I encountered passed me by, and by what strange coincidence I seemed to catch the eye of every woman. Then it was a new and quaint experience to be bawled at and addressed with strange epithets by a cabman as I crossed the road, or to be beckoned into a secluded corner by a seedy stranger and offered a pawn ticket at a knock-down price. I surmised dimly that I should probably pay for the entertainment before the evening was out, but meanwhile I found the experience quite amusing, even when I collided with a butcher who happened to be looking in the opposite direction, and who informed me with a wealth of allegory that I was "a fat-headed dude," and that I ought not to go abroad without a tin-pot and a dog.

With such pleasing adventures was the journey beguiled between Fetter Lane and the neighbourhood of Regent's Park, in which locality, at eight o'clock precisely, I mounted the doorstep of Mr Moses McDougal and rang the bell.

After some trifling delay the door was opened by a buxom and decidedly handsome housemaid who seemed to be of a cheerful and amiable temperament, for she saluted me, with a smile which struck me as exceeding the necessities of her office.

"My name," said I, "is Sidley – "

"Get along" said she; "you don't say so." I stared at her in consternation, on which she smiled more broadly than ever, and finally shattered my self-possession into impalpable fragments by finishing up with an undeniable wink.

"You needn't stand on the doorstep," said she. "Mo's having his dinner, but he won't be long. Come in and sit down in the drawing-room."

I stepped falteringly into the hall and was about to explain my business, when the housemaid, having softly shut the door, reduced me to utter stupefaction by creeping close up to me and saying in a wheedling tone:

"Aren't you going to give me a kiss?"

You could have knocked me down with a feather. You could indeed. I had no idea such things were possible. For some moments

I could do nothing but stare in speechless amazement and horror at that brazen creature. But her next remark recalled me to my present position.

"You don't seem yourself tonight," said she; "is anything the matter?"

This wouldn't do at all. I had got to be "myself" at all costs, and if "myself" was in the habit of kissing good-looking housemaids, well –

I applied my lips modestly to her forehead.

"Oh, my!" she exclaimed. "Do be careful. I should think you've been practising on your grandmother" (this baggage evidently knew a thing or two).

"Do you want me to tell Mo you're here?"

"No," I replied hurriedly, anxious to get to business and conclude this bewildering interview – for there was obviously no need for me to concern myself about the alibi – "I've just brought this umbrella back and I want my stick, that's all. Only mind you don't forget to tell Mr McMoses that I've been."

I handed her the umbrella which she carried away to the other end of the hall, returning immediately with a stick which I recognized as Charlie's.

"There," she said, "there's your stick, and now, what are you going to say for it?"

I mumbled nervously that I was much obliged but she interrupted me scornfully.

"That isn't the way you usually say thank you. What's the matter with you tonight? You haven't gone Methody, have you?"

I pulled myself together, and, trying to remember Charlie's method of salutation – when I let him – was proceeding to execute a quite creditable imitation, when the dining-room door opened very softly and there protruded a head which I instantly recognized as that of Mr McDougal by its strong likeness to the traditional portraits of Nebuchadnezzar.

"Ah!" said Moses; "so you're at it again! Come in, Mr Sidley, and you just take yourself off, you hussy!"

I was absolutely petrified. For some moments I stood like a stark imbecile, staring at the Pentateuchal countenance of Charlie's victim, while the housemaid retired with a springy step and a sort of sinuous waggle that might have meant defiance of her employer or encouragement to me.

"Don't lie shy, Mr Sidley," said the Hebrew. "I'm quite used to your little ways, you know. Won't you come in?"

"Thank you, no," I replied hurriedly. "I've just brought back your umbrella. Can't stay just now."

The door opened a little more widely and Mr McDougall slowly emerged into the hall.

"Come in just for a minute," said he. "I want to have a few words with you."

Here was a pretty state of things! If I could only get away now the alibi was perfect. But, if that wily-faced Semite once managed to lure me into the room I knew I was lost. My interview with the housemaid had convinced me of that.

"Sorry I can't stay," I spluttered, backing towards the street door. "I've got a train to catch, you know."

"But I won't keep you a minute," said Shylock, creeping after me. "I only just want half a dozen words with you."

"It's impossible," I gasped, "quite impossible. Shall lose my train."

Here I made a dash for the street door, and, having opened it, was just slipping out, when Mr McDougal rushed forward and seized the tail of my jacket.

"You've got to come back and hear what I want to tell you," he exclaimed, disregarding my protests and holding on like grim death. Evidently Mr Shylock was a gentleman who knew his own mind, and by the tone of his voice I gathered that he was somewhat short tempered.

"I'll call on you some other evening. Mr Shy – Mo –" I exclaimed with growing agitation, straining at my coat-tail, and gradually towing him across the doorstep, to the surprise and gratification of a telegraph boy, who halted on the pavement to honour us with his attention.

"I tell you you've got to come in," said Moses in a tone of dogged resolve; but at this moment my coat-tail slipped from his grasp, with the result that I shot forward like a stone from a catapult, leaving him seated on the doorstep.

But he didn't sit there very long. In a moment he was up and evidently in a towering rage, for, as I bustled away down the street, I heard him pattering behind and bawling to me to come back, on which, of course, I only walked the faster. And then the old brute began shouting to chance wayfarers to stop me and the little fiend of a telegraph boy, who had attended us closely, took up the cry in his disgusting little treble.

Then, what little nerve I had left deserted me, and as I turned the first corner, I broke into a run. Of course that was a fatal thing to do. Before you could say knife, I had a hahooing crowd at my heels, at least, not quite at my heels, because I got a good start and kept it. When I do run I run pretty fast, though I can't keep it up very long, having a slight tendency to plumpness, notwithstanding my slim figure. However, on this occasion, I sprinted forward at a fine pace, urged on by ever-increasing terror, and rather widening the distance between myself and my pursuers.

Suddenly, as I flew round a corner, my agonized eyes fell upon the words "Jacob Street." The name came to me familiarly for it was the street in which Mr Paul Everard lived. It was strange that I should have remembered it so distinctly and stranger still that I should actually, in that moment of agony, remember that his number was 63. But I did, and in the very instant that the recollection flashed on me, I saw the number painted above what looked like the entrance to a factory. The premises had a wide wooden gate in which was a small wicket, and as I approached, the aforesaid wicket began to open. Without a moment's thought, I flung myself at it, and as I fell through, slammed it behind me, and a moment later found myself sprawling on the ground in a flagged passage, held in the vice-like grip of a half-seen man, who silently thumped me as though his arm were worked by some extremely powerful kind of clockwork.

Expectation, aided by a very dirty gas lamp, enabled me to recognize Mr Paul Everard, recognition being assisted by the characteristically businesslike way in which he hammered me. I hastened to make myself known.

"There, that'll do, Mr Everard!" I exclaimed, endeavouring to wriggle out of reach; "I shall be black and blue."

He paused in the midst of a half-completed thump to examine my face and then muttering, "Rowden, by Jove!" scrambled to his feet, laughing.

"What an excitable chap you are," he said, helping me up; "can't you call on a chum without shooting in like a harlequin and knocking him down?"

"I'm awfully sorry," I said apologetically, which I certainly was for more reasons than one, "but I was in rather a hurry."

"You rather gave me that impression," Everard replied, with a grin; "but I'm glad you've looked me up."

"I hadn't really come to call on you," I said, and then noting his look of rather displeased surprise, I began to explain the circumstances as far as I could without giving Charlie away too much.

"Well," he said, "you are an extraordinary fellow, Rowden. You seem to be always in hot water, but I don't see what the deuce you ran away for. However, it's no use going into that. Are you coming in to have a yarn?"

"No, I won't come in tonight," said I. "I must get home as soon as the coast is clear."

"I expect it's clear now," said he, "but, as an extra precaution, we'd better change hats and you can put on this inverness cape of mine."

I adopted his suggestion gratefully, though the results were not all that might have been desired. The cape was well enough, though it nearly swept the ground, and his hat, considered as a disguise, was highly efficient, inasmuch as it extinguished my head completely. But from his point of view, the change was less satisfactory. You can't get a football into a pillbox.

We made our way eastward by way of quiet by-streets, in one of which we changed back once more into our proper habiliments, and during the walk little was said. I could not help being surprised at Everard's strange lack of curiosity concerning my affairs and found myself wondering if men were usually so conveniently uninterested in their fellows. At length we reached Fleet Street, and turning up Clifford's Inn Passage, entered the precincts of the Inn, where Everard looked about him with evident approval.

"So this is where you live, Rowden," he remarked. "What a delightful old place. Every corner of it is a picture, especially in this light."

I was glad that he liked my residence, but at the moment his admiration of the place caused me considerable embarrassment. Of course I ought to have asked him in, but as the rooms were still totally empty this was impossible. So I proceeded to excuse myself as well as I could, explaining that I had only just moved in and had not yet settled down.

"Very well, old chap," he said cheerfully; "I'll wait until you've fixed yourself up, and meantime I shall expect you to look in at Jacob Street in the course of a day or two."

We shook hands opposite Mr Philip Rowden's entry and I betook myself up the stairs to the empty chambers, from the window of which I watched Everard prowling about the Inn, evidently enjoying the picturesque effects of light and shade at the lamp-lit corners and the dark, mysterious entries. At length, he took himself off and I was able to creep down the stairs and sneak round to my own chambers, where, as I prepared my frugal supper, I meditated with renewed surprise upon the mysterious conduct of Mr McDougal. The behaviour of that guileless Israelite was perfectly incomprehensible to me, and so it remained until a couple of nights later when my scallywag cousin called on me and solved the mystery.

"Well, Charlie," I said, "did you collect that bill?"

He grinned a little sheepishly. "I should have done," said he, "only it wasn't there. You see, that silly ass of a pal of mine had been and paid up without telling me. So I had my trouble for nothing, and so had you, for that matter."

But in this Charlie was mistaken. I had got a little more for my trouble than he supposed, and I was going to get a little more for it than I had supposed myself.

But you will hear about that on some other occasion.

FLIGHT FOUR

A Variety Entertainment

I quite understand that one cannot fairly sneak out of the responsibility for one's own actions. That is perfectly clear. But on the other hand, I do assert and will maintain that people who deliberately expose one to temptation ought to be made to share that responsibility. Whereas they do nothing of the kind.

There was the Reverend Samuel Snoobody, for instance. Now why should he be allowed to stick up outside his conventicle a huge poster with scarlet letters announcing his intention to give an address "to young men only"? I say that such a thing ought not to be permitted. It is offering a most unwarrantable temptation to any self-respecting girl with a spark of imagination or the faintest glimmer of intelligent interest in humanity.

As to me, I don't mind admitting that I was positively devoured by curiosity. What on earth could this Snoobody person be going to say to those young men? And who were they that they should have mysterious things said to them that no one else must hear? I stood and stared hungrily at the poster as I asked myself these questions, and I should, no doubt, have stood there longer had not an elderly person of somewhat rakish aspect, who had also stopped to read the poster, taken up a position so close to me that his elbow touched mine. And even this I did not notice at first, but when the pressure of the elbow gradually increased, in spite of my drawing away from him, I realized the situation, and with one brief, indignant stare, took myself off.

What a pest to solitary girls are these superannuated roysterers who cannot be made to understand that they are on the retired list! I have no patience with them. Now, for a young man one can make some allowances, especially if his personal appearance is satisfactory – only they don't do this sort of thing; but when it comes to a grey-headed, broken-kneed old sinner, with one foot in the cat's-meat-barrow, so to speak – but there! I am letting my temper run away with me. All I have to say is that I should just like to give an address to old men only. I'd tell them a few plain truths.

But that poster haunted me. As I walked home I found myself again and again debating the question: What *could* that Snoobody creature be going to say to these young men? And it wasn't mere idle curiosity. In a way I was a sort of specialist in young men, having passed as one myself, and it seemed as if I had a legitimate interest in Mr Snoobody's remarks. However, it was clearly impossible for me to go and hear him. They wouldn't have let me in, and even if they would – well, of course, it wasn't to be thought of.

And yet – here the tempter whispered his pernicious suggestion – wasn't it? Was there not a young gentleman named Philip Rowden who might fit me with a cap of invisibility? It was, as I have said, a most pernicious suggestion and I ought to have rejected it instantly. But I didn't. On the contrary, I let the idea simmer in my mind and – well, the long and short of it is that on the following afternoon, which was the day of Mr Snoobody's address, I put aside my wig, combed my hair, slipped into a suit of Charlie's, and, popping through the loft into the chambers next door, came forth in the character of Mr Rowden.

I don't know whether young men are a chronically exhilarated class. If they are they conceal the fact successfully. As for me, I can only say that as I strode along the Strand in my neat suit and smart billycock, swinging my walking-stick and glancing knowingly into the windows of the male outfitters' shops, I felt the most delightful sense of adventurous freedom. And what pleased me most was the way in which the women looked at me. I had no idea that girls were in the habit of ogling strange young men in that fashion. I'm sure I never do. But they did, and I can tell you I ogled them back as jauntily as you please. And that is how the complications began.

It was at the crossing near Adam Street. I had got as far as the island and was waiting for a chance to dart over when I caught the eye of a particularly good-looking girl who was standing at the kerb. I suppose my bold glance confused her somewhat, for, just as a taxi had whisked past she stepped into the road. Now, following the taxi was a motor lorry which she hadn't noticed, but I had. She saw it when she was half-way across, but then, instead of darting forward, she hesitated, gave a little shriek and turned back. Then her foot must have slipped or something, for, in turning, she fell full length on the road.

It was horrible! My head whirls as I think of it, and only the most confused idea of what happened comes back to me. A dreadful scream of terror rang in my ears and mingled with the roar of the clattering Juggernaut that seemed to rush exultingly at its victim. The next moment I had sprung forward, caught the girl in my arms, and had just swung her clear when a terrific thump in the back sent me rolling over and over on the pavement.

For a few seconds I was completely dazed by the shock and the pain, but, as a crowd gathered round me, I hastily collected my wits and struggled to my feet, and then, somehow, found myself holding both the hands of the girl whom I had rescued and who was raising to me a pair of brimming eyes and a face as pale as ashes.

"Oh, I do hope you're not hurt much!" she exclaimed, almost with a sob.

"Not at all, thank you," I answered faintly, controlling a strong desire to sit down on the kerb. "Only just a little shaken."

Here a muscular arm was passed under mine and a pair of very alert grey eyes, appertaining to the arm, looked at me critically from under bushy grey eyebrows.

"You'd best come in with us and rest awhile," said the proprietor of the eyes, hooking my arm more securely. "My hotel is just here. Take his other arm, Althea, and don't hurry."

Very tenderly the father and daughter, as I assumed them to be, piloted me along the crowded pavement at the head of a procession of inquisitive idlers, and very willingly did I submit, for my knees were all of a tremble and I felt horribly sick and faint, notwithstanding which I managed to mumble a few enquiries as to the condition of my fair companion.

"Oh, I'm not hurt the tiniest bit, thanks to your heroism," she replied with a grateful squeeze of my arm, "but I'm afraid you are."

I endeavoured to reassure her – and myself at the same time for I felt absolutely mangled – but I think my looks must have rather belied my words.

"We'll see when we get you indoors," said my elderly friend. "Anyway, I'm your debtor for life. You've given me back my girl who was as good as lost, and she's all I have in the world that counts."

His strong, roughish voice shook a little as he said this and his arm tightened on mine. But at this moment we reached the entry of his hotel, where, after a brief journey in a lift, I presently found myself reclining at my ease on a large settee while a liveried menial opened a bottle of champagne. I had hastily declined my friend's offer to send for a doctor and would have refused the champagne, too being unused to stimulants, but he would take no denial. And he was perfectly right. The effect of the wine was miraculous. In a twinkling, as it seemed, all the feeling of faintness and shakiness vanished, and, but for a bruised back and a few dusty patches on my clothes I was not a penny the worse for my tumble.

"It's ridiculous," I said, "for me to be lolloping here as if I were half dead. I was only a little shaken. I'm all right now," and with this I made as if to rise. But my host insisted on my resting a little longer and drinking another glass of wine, and he was such a fatherly old dear and so masterful too that I didn't dream of disobeying. So there I sprawled for another ten minutes, chatting to Althea and getting quite hilarious after the second glass of wine, while my host paced restlessly up and down the room with his hands behind him and a watchful eye on the clock. Suddenly it dawned on me that I was probably hindering him from some important engagement, whereupon I sprang to my feet and began to offer profuse apologies.

"You've not delayed us in the least," said he; "indeed the boot is on the other leg. My daughter is just going out to do some shopping and I have a few calls to make. However, if you are quite recovered, you may as well let me put you down wherever you were going, and we must arrange for you to come and see us again soon."

"Yes, that we must," said Miss Althea, as soon as we come back from Paris. And for the present adieu! I've no words to thank you for risking your life for me."

The dear girl spoke with so much emotion as she pressed my hand that I was on the point of kissing her, but fortunately remembered myself in time, and having substituted a few delicately chosen compliments for the more natural demonstration, took myself off in the wake of her vanishing parent.

I have never seen a man in such a hurry or so determined to do fifty things at the same time. He reminded me of Julius Caesar, who, I understand, was in the habit of writing a letter with each hand, while he dictated a third and cast up his accounts with his toes. Well, that's the sort of person my host was. As he ambled along the endless corridors with me trotting at his heels he managed to read his engagement book, make notes and furnish me with a concentrated autobiography, as well as to assure me in the most emphatic manner that John B Potter of New York, U.S.A., was my life-long friend.

As we reached the ground floor he shot out of the lift Jack-in-the-box fashion, and darting to the telephone, began turning the handle as if he were trying to make it play a tune.

But the English telephone was one too many for him. My heart swelled with national pride as I stood by and listened.

"Hello! – Hello! – Yes – John B Potter – No, Potter – What's that? – I said Potter – Yes – about those boots, why haven't you sent them? – No! Boots – I said boots – BOOTS! – Yes – No – NO! – What's that? – well, who are you, anyway? What? Did you say Antivivisection Society? – No! – NO – That blamed girl has put me on to the wrong number!"

He seized the handle and once more whirled it round as if grinding a particularly refractory sample of coffee, soliloquizing in a low tone with a furtive eye on me. He made several new acquaintances before he finally ran the boots to earth, and meanwhile I had quite a pleasant little rest. Then he darted away from the telephone, bounced down the steps, ricochetted on to the pavement and whisked open the door of a taxi.

"Where did you say you wanted to be put down?" he asked.

The question took me by surprise. At the moment I could not recall the exact whereabouts of Mr Snoobody's establishment, and, as I had to say something I said the first thing that occurred to me, which happened to be Westminster Abbey. My host repeated the direction to the driver and away we went.

"I'll be wanting to see you again soon," Mr Potter said presently as we whirled past the Houses of Parliament and swept round towards the Abbey, "but I've just got to make a call or two at Amsterdam and Hamburg and Paris. When my girl and I get back you must come and see us. And that reminds me that I don't know your name or where to find you."

Now, of course, this was just what I might have expected; but I had been so flustered that I had not given a single thought to the question as to what name I should give if asked. Once more I was taken by surprise, and as at this moment the taxi stopped and Mr

Potter leaped out, I followed, fumbling feebly in my pocket for Mr Philip Rowden's cardcase.

"Well," Mr Potter exclaimed cheerily, "goodbye! goodbye! – or rather au revoir – for we shall meet again quite soon, I hope." He sprang into the cab, and taking from me the card that I had at length produced, slammed the door and roared the new destination out of the window. The motor gave a sort of hiccup and the cab started, leaving me with a sort of memory picture of Mr John B Potter smiling farewell to me, consulting his engagement book and reading my card at one and the same time.

I stood for some seconds at the corner, gazing at the receding taxi and slowly recovering from the strenuous companionship of my new friend. I was about to return the cardcase to my pocket when I happened to glance at it with reviving intelligence. And then I started some, as Mr Potter would have said, for it was a red morocco case. But Philip Rowden's case was of green russia. Moreover, this case bore legibly in stamped lettering the initials "C S." With trembling fingers I snatched out a card and read it, and of course, there it was: "Mr Charles Sidley, Roysterers Club, St James's Street." I had put on the wrong waistcoat and hadn't examined the pockets.

Well, the fat was in the fire now and no mistake! Whatever would Charlie say when he got the inevitable letter from Mr Potter? It was an awful affair! And yet – well, it was really a rather juicy situation, and I was out of the muddle at any rate. With which satisfactory reflection I looked at my watch and turned my steps in the direction of Mr Snoobody's establishment. But I didn't get very far. The fact is that on sober reflection I saw that the thing was impossible. The address was to young men only and I was not a young man after all. Suppose Mr Snoobody should say something that was not quite nice for a girl to hear! It would be most horrid. I hadn't thought of that.

But in any case I shouldn't have got there, for Providence stepped in and took charge of me firmly. My first steps on the road to ruin led me into a large, rambling shop to get a pair of gloves, as my own — or rather, Charlie's — had burst when I fell down. There, at the next counter, was a smart-looking woman of about thirty with a small dog and a large reticule thing full of all sorts of oddments that she had been buying. That absurd reticule amused me intensely, and so did the woman herself, she was so extremely dignified and "sidey," so much so that I was tempted when I caught her eye, to bestow on her a significant and decidedly rakish smile, on which she looked ready to burst with indignation. When I had bought my gloves I marched off to the cashier's desk, at which I arrived with several other persons at the same time as my fair friend, with whom in fact, I collided slightly, to her unspeakable wrath; and while she was paying her bill I took the opportunity to inspect the reticule. Then I paid my own bill and followed her out of the shop, when I lost sight of her — for the time.

I have mentioned that I was much interested to observe the power of the human eye (under a masculine hat) on the women whom I met, and I was pursuing certain psychological investigations along these lines when I observed a showy-looking woman approaching and proceeded to try my new powers on her. The effect in this case was a little more than I had bargained for. The subject of the experiment stopped dead, and acknowledging my insinuating half-smile with a smile and a half, darted at me with outstretched hand.

"How *do* you do, Mr Sidley?" she exclaimed.

I answered that I did very well, thank you, only I wasn't Mr Sidley.

She looked at me reproachfully through a pair of rather odd-looking pince-nez.

"I see you're still as full of your nonsense as ever," she said, and then asked, "Have you seen Winifred lately?" (Hallo! Master Charlie! Who might Winifred be? I must enquire into this.)

"Not very lately," I replied. "In fact I have no recollection of ever having seen her at all."

"Naughty boy!" exclaimed my fair friend. "Why do you talk such nonsense?"

49

"But, really, I assure you – " I began, but she cut me short.

"Now don't be so silly. You've had your little joke and I don't think much of it. Tell me what you've been doing with yourself all this time."

I was about to renew my protests when her face suddenly underwent a singular change as she stared over my shoulder. The next moment a hand touched my arm and a feminine voice said:

"That is the man."

I whisked round like lightning to find myself confronted by the woman whom I had seen in the glove shop and a diffident-looking policeman.

"What do you want?" I demanded.

"This lady," said the policeman, "accuses you of having taken a parcel out of her bag or basket or whatever it is."

"He took it out while I was paying my bill at the desk," the woman explained.

"Rubbish!" said I. "You've dropped it or the dog has eaten it."

"Nothing of the kind," she retorted. "You've stolen it."

The constable ran his eyes over me evidently assessing my capacity for concealing parcels, and asked:

"What sized parcel was it?"

"Oh, an ordinary-sized parcel, you know," she replied.

"I see," said the constable. "Ordinary-sized. Now, about how big would that be, ma'am?"

"Why about – about as big as a good-sized piece of Irish poplin folded up rather small."

"I see," said the constable, tipping his helmet forward the more conveniently to scratch the back of his head. "M'yes." Again he looked at me dubiously as if seeking some incriminating protuberance; and at this point my new acquaintance interposed.

"What preposterous nonsense!" she exclaimed indignantly. "This gentleman, constable, is a person of means and good social position, and I may say that I have known him well for years."

"I haven't, you know," said the woman with the reticule.

"I said," my friend retorted frigidly, "that he was a gentleman of position," upon which the reticule person gasped with rage and the policeman struggled unsuccessfully to conceal a smile.

"I think," said he, "I had better take your name and address. Would you give me your card?"

Would I not? I had the cardcase out in a twinkling, and it was only when I saw it open in my hand that I remembered that it was Charlie's. However, that could not be helped now. Explanations would have been fatal.

The constable took the card from me and read it aloud: " 'Mr Charles Sidley, Roysterers Club, St James's Street.' Very well, sir, we'll enquire into the matter."

But here the reticule person broke in viciously: "This won't do, constable. I insist on your taking this man into custody. He probably has the stolen property about him at this moment."

The policeman had another scratch at the back of his head and thereby produced a new idea.

"We'd better go to the shop and get a description of the parcel," said he, and regardless of the protests of my accuser we all set off together to the "scene of the crime." Our appearance there created quite a little sensation, and as we approached the counter the saleswoman watched us apprehensively, though with a faint smile of recognition.

"I suppose, Madam," said she, addressing my accuser, "you have come back for your parcel. I didn't notice that you hadn't taken it until you had left the shop." She reached down into some receptacle and bringing up a parcel about the size of a brick, laid it on the counter. My heart gave a bound of relief, my companion snorted scornfully, the policeman grinned and the reticule person, who had turned the colour of a beetroot, grabbed up the parcel and stalked out of the shop without a word.

"Well, I'm sure!" exclaimed my new acquaintance, and the constable having expressed entire concurrence in the sentiment, touched his helmet and departed.

As soon as we were outside, my friend reverted to our interrupted conversation.

"It seems a long time since I last saw you, Mr Sidley," she remarked. "Have you been away from London?"

I made one more desperate effort to escape from this absurd situation.

"You must excuse me," I said, "if I repeat once more that I am not Mr Sidley. I am really – "

But here she cut me short with some asperity of manner. "Oh, please," said she, "let us take that joke as read. It's getting a little tiresome, especially after your having given your card to the constable."

I had forgotten that beastly card. Of course it had committed me hopelessly to the identity of my scallywag cousin, and as I realized this, I became so confused that I had actually accepted an invitation to tea at her flat before I could recover myself. It was an awful mess that I had got myself into. I was certain to give myself away sooner or later unless I could escape, for, of course, I didn't even know the good woman's name. So I trudged at her side in no end of a twitter wondering how on earth I was going to get out of this scrape and letting her talk in the hope that I should at least find out who she was. Presently she turned into a quiet, narrow side street, about half-way up which was the entrance to her flat. Just as we walked into the hall the lift descended and a lady stepped out, leaving it empty.

"The lift boy is playing truant again," she remarked as we stepped in.

"So I see," my friend answered, and, giving the rope a tug she started us on our upward journey. The lift had nearly risen clear of the hall when the lady below ran to the door and called up the shaft: "Nellie Barrow is upstairs and Charlie Sidley."

My blood froze. Charlie Sidley! Now I was in for it and no mistake!

"What did she say?" my friend asked.

"Nellie Barrow and who?"

"Er – didn't quite catch it," I stammered. "Sounded rather like Charlotte Ridley."

"Ridley?" my friend repeated. "Ridley? Now who is she, I wonder. However, we shall see. Here we are." She brought the lift skilfully to the landing and, pushing open the door, stepped out. "Come along," she said.

Come along indeed! Not I. My hand was on the rope before she had fairly stepped out, and no sooner did her foot touch the landing than I gave a mighty tug. In an instant the floor fell away and the landing door shot upward giving me a momentary glimpse of my late companion's astonished face as I sank at her feet like a stage demon. I stopped the lift quite neatly at the ground floor, and, darting out, crossed the hall and in a moment was legging it – if you will pardon the expression – down the street like a runaway lamplighter, to get clear, if possible, before the avenging Charlie should have time to appear in pursuit. At the bottom of the little street, however, I met with an obstruction, and a very irritating one, too. A suffragette procession was passing and completely blocked the way.

"You can't come out yet," said a bumptious-looking little suffy who seemed to be a sort of official. "You must wait until we've passed."

This didn't suit me at all, for Charlie was probably on my heels at this very moment, so, without replying, I just helped her out of the way with my elbow. I suppose my elbow must have hurt her, for she gave a howl and smacked my face quite hard; and such was my confusion of mind that, forgetting my disguise, I smacked her in return, a good deal harder. The instant I had done it I saw what a fatal mistake I had made, but it was too late then.

My word! what a phillaloo arose. It sounded like a sort of diabolic litany of which the words "brute" and "coward" formed the unending refrain. The suffies surged around me, pushing, pinching and clawing, and, what was much more alarming, a big, half-baked-looking man with a little fluffy beard and a red necktie, handed his ridiculous banner to a woman and began to bear down on me. I was most horridly frightened and no doubt I showed it; and the more frightened I became, the more warlike he grew. Frantically I elbowed my way through the crowd of women by which I had been borne along, until at last I got clear, and fairly bolting off along the pavement, darted up the first turning that I came to. And here I made another fatal error; for no sooner had I entered the turning than I realized with horror that it was the very street that I had just escaped from.

For one moment I halted in absolute despair, then observing an open doorway close by, I darted in and found myself in a sort of lobby or waiting-room attached to some offices, and providentially empty at the moment. And I was none too soon, for my first glance out of the window through the wire blind showed me, on the one hand, a little crowd of suffies headed by the warrior with the red tie, and on the other, my respected cousin, standing just outside the flat, looking up and down the street as he rolled a cigarette.

I watched eagerly for the inevitable catastrophe. Up the little street marched the red-tied warrior with his little band of undersized amazons, nearer and nearer to the unconscious Charlie, until at last –

Smack! That was the warrior's open hand on my worthy cousin's face, and you never saw anyone look so utterly astounded as Charlie did. For one moment he stood as if he were petrified, but only for one moment. The next he – well, I don't know how to describe it, it was so confusing. Charlie looked like one of those Indian gods that are all over arms and legs, and the warrior began to run backwards quite fast, treading on the toes of the suffies as he came, and followed closely by Charlie, and when he sat down on the kerb to attend to his nose with a red and white handkerchief, the suffies whose toes he had trodden on gathered round and gibbered at him. But they were quite civil to Charlie.

Then a couple of policemen appeared and began to move them on. And at this moment a sour-faced elderly man came out of the office and addressed himself to me.

"Yes?"

"Oh," said I, rather flustered and, as usual, unprepared, "er – let me see – isn't this the office of the – ha – hm – the Society for the – er – amelioration of the – ha – conditions of – er – of Repentant Hebrews?"

"No, it isn't," he said crisply.

"Oh, indeed," said I with a furtive eye on the retreating suffies. "Can you tell me where the Society's offices are?"

"No, I can't," he replied.

"Oh, really!" said I. "How unfortunate! But perhaps you have a directory in which one might find the address?"

"No, I haven't," said he.

"Then do you know anyone who could let me see one?"

"No, I don't," he answered.

By this time the street was clear and the harbour of refuge no longer required. Accordingly I thanked the office person, and wishing him good afternoon, stole out warily. Policeman, warrior, suffies and Charlie had all vanished leaving me to go my way in peace.

On my way home, near Westminster Bridge, I dropped in at a tea shop for a little rest and a cup of coffee. But I had not been settled in my shady corner more than five minutes when two persons came in at the opposite entrance and gave me such a start that I nearly dropped my cup. You will hardly believe me when I tell you that one of them was Charlie and the other the little suffy whom I had smacked. And they were as thick as thieves, too, for I watched them practising palmistry across the table while they were waiting for their tea.

Well, well. We can't all follow the counsels of perfection, but still, as I sneaked out of the back entrance and took my way homeward, I reflected on that suffy and Mr Shylock's housemaid and the mysterious Winifred and the rest of the unknown but suspected repertoire – like even unto that of Solomon in all his glory – and made a mental note that Charlie would have to be content to shake hands in future.

FLIGHT FIVE

A Double Capture

When the curtain was rung down on the last scene of my little drama, the character who occupied the stage and engrossed the modest beam of limelight was my cousin Charlie; and as the curtain rises on the present scene it is that same scallywag who is the first to respond to the call-boy's summons.

The summons of that call-boy, whom we mortals name Fate or Destiny, was inaudible to me. Charlie's response was not inaudible. Not at all. By no means. Not in the least. Certainly not. But I had better proceed to straightforward narration.

It was about four o'clock in the afternoon. I was sitting at my window, stitching industriously at a pretty little bedroom curtain, when I became aware of soft footsteps on my stair. Instantly I popped the curtain into a drawer and took out an unfinished blouse. Not that there is anything incriminating about a bedroom curtain, only I was making it for my next door neighbour, Mr Philip Rowden, and as I didn't want to – but you know all about Mr Rowden, so I needn't worry you with explanations.

Well, the footsteps continued to ascend, rather stealthily. And then I heard another step on the stair – Charlie's, unmistakably, and not at all stealthy. The two sets of footsteps met, so to speak, somewhere on the top flight, and then I heard someone speaking softly, and then I heard Charlie's voice, not speaking softly. I could hear what he said quite plainly but I would rather not repeat it, if you don't mind. He was being rude to somebody – awfully rude. And he was so fluent, too! I can't imagine where he picked up such expressions.

Well, there was a short pause then and the next thing that I heard was a sound like that which a strenuous fishmonger might make in laying down a stale halibut on a marble slab; and then there was a most horrid noise – just as if a half-dozen or so intoxicated bullocks were hurrying down the stairs to catch a train. It was an awful hubbub. It positively shook the house. But it gradually died away in the distance, by which I judged that Charlie and his friend were getting near the bottom of the stairs and would presently come out of the entry into the courtyard. And so they did. I had hardly taken my place at the window when a very shiny silk hat shot out of the entry with the most surprising velocity. And then Charlie and his friend came out.

Now, just opposite my window, in the middle of the small courtyard, is a lamppost with the dearest, quaintest old lamp that you ever saw. Well, Charlie's friend seemed to want to get to that lamp-post and I must say that Charlie helped him all he could, and how he managed to keep his balance while he was doing it I can't think. However, he did get to the lamp-post accompanied by Charlie – and then he began to go round it quite quickly – still accompanied by Charlie. And at that moment, as he turned his face towards me, I saw, to my utter astonishment that Charlie's friend was the foreign person who had followed me to the National Gallery and as I more than suspect, set those wretches on to kidnap me.

I recognized him in an instant. And it was fortunate that I did, for by the time he had gone round that lamp-post a dozen times or so he wasn't nearly so easy to recognize. There seemed to be something wrong with one of his eyes – a sort of darkness of the skin, you know – and he kept it shut for some reason, and he seemed quite excited, too, which I suppose was natural under the circumstances, and so was Charlie, for that matter.

Well, presently the foreign gentleman appeared to get tired of the lamp-post (and it was monotonous, you must admit, going round the same lamp-post so many times), for he darted across towards the Fetter Lane gate. But even then Charlie didn't desert him (he is an awfully constant fellow, is Charlie, I will say that for him), and, as the foreign gentleman seemed to have forgotten his hat, Charlie very thoughtfully brought it along with him. Of course there wasn't time to pick it up, but Charlie is an excellent football player. Judging by the curve the hat described, it will probably have descended on the other side of Fetter Lane.

I was sorry when the two friends disappeared. It is hateful to see two people knocking one another about – but still, if they *must* do it, why they may as well chose a place where it is possible for an interested party to get a fairly good view of the proceedings. However, I comforted myself with the reflection that Charlie would come back presently, when he had given his name and address to the police, and then I should hear the full details of the interview. And, sure enough, he did come back, in about ten minutes, looking a little warm and ruffled but quite calm and evidently very pleased with himself. But, instead of proceeding at once to satisfy my natural curiosity, he began to talk about some silly dramatic entertainment for which he had got tickets. It was the sort of stupid thing that a man *would* do, but I wasn't going to be put off in that way.

"Never mind about the dramatic show, Charlie." said I. "Tell me about this other little show. Why were you thumping that foreign person in such an obstreperous fashion?"

Charlie looked at me vacantly. "Foreign person?" said he. "What foreign person?"

"Oh, rats!" I exclaimed impatiently (I picked up that elegant expression from Charlie himself). "Do you think I'm deaf or blind? I heard you go down the stairs and I saw you chasing him round the lamp-post."

"You had no business to look," he said, severely.

"Well, I did, and I want to know what it was all about."

At this, Charlie put on a peculiarly mulish expression.

"Now, look here, Phyl," he said sourly, "don't you be so beastly inquisitive. It's no affair of yours."

Oh, wasn't it? That was all he knew. But of course, I couldn't explain, so I just said, very meekly: "I'm not inquisitive, Charlie. I only want to know all about it."

"Don't see the difference," said he. "And to return to this dramatic – "

"I'm not going to return to it," I exclaimed. "I want to know why you were thumping that foreigner."

Charlie looked just as if he had swallowed something nasty by mistake, and he glared at me as if I had given it to him.

"Can't you understand, Phyl," said he "that there are certain things that a man doesn't talk about to a girl?"

Of course I did. And I also understood that those were precisely the things that a girl is most ravenously inquisitive about. That last question of his finished me. I had got either to know or burst. And I wasn't going to burst.

"I quite understand, Charlie," I replied in a gentle but slightly shocked tone. "Forgive me for bothering you. We all have our little skeletons in our little cupboards, and I won't try to peep into yours. The world is full of temptations, my dear boy, and I don't suppose you are worse than other people. At any rate, I never took you for an angel, Charlie, so you will be just the same to me."

That fetched him. I knew it would. Not that I take any credit for the little stratagem. Every girl knows the sort of worsted mayfly that will bring a man popping up, open-mouthed, out of his native element. Charlie came up like a hungry trout and was on the hook before you could say "Moses."

"You're quite mistaken, Phyl," he spluttered. "This isn't any racket of mine. Only I didn't want to talk about it because one doesn't like women to know what beasts some men are. Still, if you are going to suspect me, I must tell you exactly what happened, but I'll be hanged if I understand what it meant."

"This is what happened: I was coming up your stair when I overtook this foreign devil and tried to pass him, but he caught hold of my arm and began to talk a parcel of infernal balderdash."

"What sort?" I asked coaxingly.

"Well, he begged me not to be so coy – me coy, you know, Phyl!"

"Yes, indeed!" I murmured, thinking of Mr Shylock's housemaid.

"And he asked me why I always avoided him when he loved me so passionately – never saw the brute before in my life – and a lot more tommy rot of that sort."

"And what did you say?"

"I told him to go back to his native asylum and put himself in a padded cell. And then, if you'll believe me, the brute tried to kiss me!"

"Tried to what, Charlie?" I gasped.

"To kiss me!" shouted Charlie. "Put his beastly arm round my neck and shoved his dirty muzzle close to my face! I assure you, Phyl – "

But at this point I exploded. For a moment or two, sheer, incredulous amazement had kept me silent, but as the preposterous reality burst upon me, I fell back in my chair and laughed until tears of joy trickled down my cheeks and I felt a distinct threatening of hiccups.

"I don't see what the deuce you've got to laugh at," Charlie said, looking at me with glum disapproval.

"I beg your pardon, Charlie," I said unsteadily. "It *was* rude and silly of me to laugh. But you needn't look at me like that. Anyone would think that I had tried to kiss you."

"Would they?" he replied, with a grin. "They'd be precious bad judges if they did."

As he showed a tendency to rise from his chair, I hastily reverted to the encounter.

"And what did you do?" I asked.

"Do!" he exclaimed. "Why I fetched him a wipe across the snout that helped him down the first flight and then I booted him down the other two. You saw the rest of the interview. We exchanged farewells in Fetter Lane just outside the gate."

"I wonder he didn't give you in charge for assault."

"Do you?" said Charlie. "I don't. A pretty figure he'd cut in a police court. No, Phyl, not much. But he hinted at an intention of settling the score another way, and I have no doubt he'll keep his word. You ought to have seen the look he gave me. I tell you, the devil would be quite a pleasant-looking fellow by comparison."

"I shouldn't think he'll want to have any further dealings with you," said I.

But Charlie shook his head. "Not personally," said he. "It will be a proxy job and it won't be a matter of knuckles. You don't know these dagoes, Phyl. It's difficult for an English person to realize the lengths they will go to satisfy a grudge. However, I'm not taking it lying down. I shall make my little arrangements, too. Mr Browning's establishment is only just over the way. I shall look in there presently and fit myself out with the latest thing in pop-guns, and then my benevolent friends can mind their eye. But now, to go back to that dramatic show. I should like you to come, Phyl, because the chappie who wrote the play is a friend of mine."

"I should like to come very much," said I.

"Very well, then," he rejoined, "I'll give you a ticket, though I expect I shall be able to come and take you to the place. But don't wait for me, in case I can't come, and if you go by yourself, take a cab, because the neighbourhood isn't quite a nice one for a girl to walk through alone. My pal couldn't afford one of the regular repertory theatres and this one is all right when you're inside, but the locality is a bit shady, to say the least, so mind you take a cab. But I expect I shall be able to call for you."

Shortly after this Charlie took his departure, leaving me just a little uncomfortable at the thought of the danger that lurked in his path. He was not a nervous man who was likely to exaggerate that danger, and, indeed, my own experiences told me how correctly he had judged the desperate character of that foreign person. It was a pity that circumstances prevented me from telling him all I knew and so putting him further on his guard. But that was clearly impossible, and there was nothing for it but to hope for the best, which I did, and in my rather irresponsible way, soon more or less completely forgot both the incident itself and the vaguely threatening danger.

When the evening of the dramatic entertainment arrived I so far followed Charlie's instructions that instead of waiting for him I set forth rather unnecessarily early. But here my obedience ended. Disregarding the procession of empty hansoms that crawled down Fleet Street, I betook myself briskly to Ludgate Circus, and then, impelled by some demon of perverseness, started in the gathering dusk to walk towards Blackfriars Bridge. I am not fond of cabs and I am very fond of the inexhaustible London streets, and a "shady" neighbourhood seemed to offer an alluring prospect from the standpoint of the explorer.

It was all plain sailing as far as the obelisk at the bottom of the Blackfriars Road, but after that I got into rather a muddle. I walked up one street and down another, very much interested in the queer squalid neighbourhood and its curious population, but gradually becoming more and more obscure as to where I was. At last, beginning to fear that I should be late for the entertainment, I stopped in a quiet, empty-looking street, and looked round. A respectable-looking man, who carried an overcoat on his arm, was approaching, and a little way behind him a four-wheeled cab was crawling by the kerb. I accosted the man who instantly halted and raised his hat respectfully.

"Can you tell me which is the shortest way to Montrose Square?" I asked.

The man considered for a moment, and then answered, with a slight foreign accent:

"It is some little distance from here, Miss, and there is a rather bad neighbourhood to cross in getting to it. If I might presume to advise, it would be better for a young lady like you to take a cab. I see there is one coming which seems to be empty; shall I call to him to stop?"

It did certainly seem to be the best thing to do, seeing that I was already rather late and might easily lose my way again. Accordingly I said "yes" and thanked the man who at once hailed the cab and escorted me towards it. The driver was evidently pleased at getting a fare, for he climbed down from his box to hold the door open for me. I gave him the direction and was just stepping into the cab when the man dexterously flung his overcoat over my head, and, gripping my arms at the elbows, pushed me forward so that I fell on my knees on the floor. Immediately the door was slammed behind me, and a couple of seconds later I felt the cab move on.

I was horribly frightened, and needless to say, I struggled with all my might. But it was of no use. I was perfectly helpless. The coat was drawn so tightly round my head that I was nearly suffocated, and jammed as I was down in the corner of the cab with that villain's arms clasping mine tightly to my sides, I was quite unable to move. And then I felt the wretch's hands move stealthily round my waist, though without loosening his grip on my arms, and presently I felt a cord passed once or twice around me, just below my elbows. I made one more frantic struggle to free myself, but just then the cord tightened, pinioning my arms immovably to my sides. And meanwhile the cab rumbled on at quite a rapid pace.

The journey was not a long one. I can say that much, though, of course, I have no idea of the direction that we took. My efforts to call out were as futile as my struggles, for the overcoat was pressed so closely against my mouth that I had much ado to breathe, and presently my captor secured it still more closely with one or two turns of cord or string round my head so that I was effectually gagged, and finally the wretch tied my ankles together.

It was just after the perpetration of this last atrocity that we reached our destination. The cab stopped and gave a sideways jolt as the driver sprang down from the box, the door opened and I was hauled out, struggling feebly and uttering muffled cries. The two men carried me quickly across a narrow pavement and into a small passage, as I judged by the sound of their feet upon a wooden floor; a door slammed behind us and then I felt myself being carried up a flight of stairs and into a room, where I was deposited on the floor.

" 'Ere she is, mister," I heard a voice say – apparently that of the cabman. "A bloomin' neat cop, I calls it, and a rare old job it was, a-follerin' of 'er all the way from Fleet Street with that there cab."

"Uncover her head and let us see that you've caught the right bird," said another and more refined voice, and evidently not an English one.

"She'll 'oller if yer do," said the cabman.

"It is no matter," was the reply. "We will put on the gag."

Thereupon the cord around my head was unfastened and the overcoat twitched off, and but for the little scarf that I had put over my head and tied under my chin, my wig would have been twitched off with it. Oddly enough, I noted the fact, half-unconsciously, at the time, although my attention was pretty well occupied otherwise. I had felt from the first very little doubt as to whose hands I had fallen into, and the instant my eyes were uncovered, my worst suspicions were verified. It is really superfluous for me to mention that the third man was the foreign person who had suffered so severely from Charlie's righteous indignation.

As soon as my eyes lighted on him, I uttered a piercing shriek. But only one. For, in an instant, the cabman had his hand over my mouth and held it there until his fellow ruffian was able to slip a disgusting gag into its place, by which my breathing was so much hindered that I was unable to utter a sound.

"Was she alone when you caught her, Jacob?" the foreign wretch asked.

"Yes, quite alone. She walked into the net almost of her own accord."

"And where are the others?" the foreign villain asked.

"I don't know. Marcovitz said something about getting a covered van, and he went off with Briedmann, so Isaacs and I got the cab out and kept a watch on the Fetter Lane gate. Perhaps the others are watching the other gate."

"I hope they will be careful," said the arch-villain. "We don't want them followed here, especially now that I have succeeded in inducing my beautiful young friend to accept my humble hospitality."

As he uttered these last words, he came over to where I was sitting on the floor with my back against the wall and leered at me in a way that made my flesh creep. I have never seen a more horribly evil-looking wretch. The other two mere commonplace brutes were quite pleasant by comparison. And of course, Charlie's little attentions had not improved his appearance, though the traces of that one-sided battle were not very conspicuous, since the room was lighted only by a paraffin lamp that stood on a sort of rough sideboard. Still, I could see enough to give me such a sinking at the heart as I had never before known in the whole of my life.

"You are a very beautiful girl, my dear," he said, with a hideous smile, "but that gag does not become you any more than those male clothes that you wore on another occasion that you may remember. We must manage to do without the gag. We must learn to keep our pretty mouth shut excepting to say pretty things."

Here he gave a soft, horrible chuckle and glanced towards his two familiar demons who had by this time edged towards the sideboard, with evident interest in the bottles and glasses that were displayed on it. He was about to resume his diabolical facetiousness when a loud clatter arose from below and a door slammed heavily.

"Now what the devil can that be?" he exclaimed, stepping over to the door and opening it. "Who is there?"

"It's us," a voice responded. "Marcovitz and Briedmann. We've got her!"

"Got her!" repeated the arch-demon.

"Got who? This is some accursed stupidity. But we shall see."

We did see, very shortly, when the two villains — a tall, beady-eyed Pole and a squab-faced German Jew — staggered into the room, carrying a long packing case.

"Rather neat, senor, hm?" chuckled the Pole, as they set the case down on the floor; but at this moment his eyes fell on me and he stopped with his mouth agape.

"Ha!" he exclaimed in a dismayed tone, "but is it that there are two of them?"

The arch-devil gave a horrid grin. "Open the case, open the case," he commanded impatiently, "and let us see what you have caught."

The two men hastily untied a cord and threw off the loose lid of the case, whereupon like some dreadful jack-in-the-box, up rose the head and shoulders of my poor cousin Charlie. It was just what I had feared, and evidently what the arch-devil had hoped, for he greeted the apparition with a howl of joy.

"Ah!" he screamed, "it is my dear friend! I have longed to see him once more. And now he is here, under my poor roof. How joyful shall I be to entertain him! To keep him amused with our little playful diversions. Jacob, my friend, where is that beautiful hippo-hide whip?"

"Downstairs," grunted Jacob, with a thirsty glance at the bottles.

"Good," said the arch-devil. "Presently we will bring it up. The hippopotamus, dear friend," he continued, with a diabolic leer at Charlie "is a thick-skinned animal; the Englishman is also a thick-skinned animal. But I think the skin of the hippo — however, we shall see."

To all this, of course, poor Charlie answered not a word, for his mouth, like mine, was covered by a gag; and it was evident from the rigid way in which he sat up that he was bound hand and foot. When his head had first risen from the case he had been crimson with wrath, but when he saw me, his face went as pale as ashes, poor boy! And even now, ignoring his tormentor, he kept his eyes fixed on me with a look of unutterable horror and pity.

"So," resumed the arch-devil, " we are quite a little family party. Your charming sister will, by and by, visit, under my escort, the beautiful cities of South America. Perhaps you shall come, too – part of the way, until I have finished the little entertainment that I propose for you. Then – but no doubt you are an excellent swimmer. Is it not so?" He gave a fiendish leer, and then, turning to his subordinate demons, said: "Come, my friends, you have done well. It is a brilliant exploit. We shall all drink the healths of this brave English gentleman and his charming sister. Let us fill our glasses."

The five wretches gathered by the sideboard and began to pour out the liquor into coarse-looking tumblers, while I continued to gaze in an agony of terror at my unfortunate cousin. Poor dear Charlie! To what unthinkable horrors had my indiscretions, all unconsciously, consigned him! What self-condemnation did I pronounce – quite unjustly, as I now feel, after sober reflection, but then –

Suddenly I became aware that Charlie was making secret, but rather obvious signs to some invisible person, who would seem to be hiding behind what I had taken to be the half-open door of a cupboard. He nodded and grimaced and smiled over his gag in a most singular manner, and I trembled lest he should be observed before he had conveyed his meaning to the – presumably friendly – unknown. And observed he very soon was. Marcovitz noticed him first, and his exclamation drew the attention of the others, who all gazed in astonishment, first at Charlie and then at the door, towards which Marcovitz stole on tip-toe. Apparently he saw nothing there and said so and then the five wretches turned to stare at Charlie, and so did I, and –

Ye gods! What a change in the situation! Charlie wasn't smiling at all now! Grim as fate was my worthy cousin's face. And somehow – I couldn't imagine how – his arms had slipped out of his bonds and both his hands were raised. One of them was engaged in pulling down the gag and the other held the funniest looking pistol that you ever saw.

"Hands up all!" said Charlie. "I shoot the first man that moves."

Four pairs of hands went up, rather undecidedly, but Marcovitz thrust one of his under the skirt of his coat. Then a jet of violet flame darted from Charlie's pistol, there was a horrid, sharp report that hurt my ears, and Marcovitz seemed to double up and lay on the floor quite still, excepting that I noticed his hands opening and closing and that his feet shuffled to and fro in a queer sort of way.

"Next man," said Charlie. "Don't be shy, gentlemen, I shall be delighted to have a fair pretext."

But the delight was all on his side. The four pairs of hands were held aloft at the ends of rigidly extended arms, and four terrified faces glared into those menacing eyes that looked along the pistol-barrel. There was a silence of some seconds duration, broken only by the soft slithering of Marcovitz's feet. Then Charlie rose slowly from the case, keeping a grim and steady glance bent on the four cowering ruffians, and stepping out, crept across the room to me, feeling in his pocket with his free hand. As he reached me, he drew it out and held a pocket knife towards me.

"Pull out the blade, Phyl, while I hold the handle," said he.

This I managed with some difficulty to do, and as soon as the knife was opened he slipped the blade under the cord that held my arms and cut through it. My arms being now free, I took the knife from him, and having liberated my ankles, cut the string of the gag and then I rose to my feet.

At this moment the man Jacob, who was standing near the lamp, turned quickly and blew down the chimney. In an instant, the room was in darkness, and in the next instant it was lighted up by a violet flash and the sharp report seemed to mingle with the sound of a heavy fall and a loud, bubbling groan.

"Outside, Phyl!" exclaimed Charlie, and grasping my arm he hustled me through the doorway out on to the landing and down the stairs, following me as I could feel, with his back towards me and his face towards the door which he had closed behind him. We both stepped quietly, so that we should hear any sounds of pursuit, and soon reached the narrow hall, along which I groped while he covered the retreat. I soon had the door open and then we both darted out into the street, where at the kerb, Mr Isaac's cab was still waiting in charge of a small boy, who at the sight of Charlie's face and the queer-looking pistol, made off in terror.

"Jump in, Phyl," said Charlie, opening the door of the cab, and as I sprang in, he climbed to the box and caught the horse such a swipe with the whip that it bounded forward like a frightened antelope and then settled down to a furious gallop. This was an excellent start, for in a few seconds we had left our late prison far behind, but it had its disadvantages, as Charlie discovered when he ceased to look back with his pistol pointed along the roof, and tried to manipulate the reins. For the horse had fairly bolted and continued to gallop furiously up the dark street regardless of Charlie's efforts.

It was certainly rough travelling, especially after we passed a lamp-post rather too near, and left one of our hind wheels behind. But the journey was not a long one. It ended – as to its vehicular character – at the entrance to a widish court which formed the continuation of the street, which entrance was guarded by a couple of massive posts.

That horse of ours was a rank egotist, a perfectly self-centred beast who thought of nothing but himself. And thus, gauging the distance between the posts, concluded that there was room enough for him to pass. And so there was, but of course, when it came to the cab – well, Charlie had seen what was coming, and jammed himself against the foot-board, so he was able to climb down and pull me out through the window before the spectators collected. Then we hurried up the court, and quite soon we came out into the Mile End Road (where we noticed a crowd gathered around a horse and an overturned sarsaparilla stall), and here we got into a Blackwall omnibus bound westward.

Charlie was very silent and serious in the omnibus and I forbore to interrupt his thoughts. I judged that he was thinking of those two men, whom he had killed, and I suppose it is a rather solemn and dreadful thing to have to take the lives even of such wretches as those, though, personally, I felt quite indifferent about it. Still, Charlie's conscience might easily be more tender than mine and it was proper for me to respect his feelings, which I did, and neither of us spoke until we had got down by St Dunstan's Church and were walking up Clifford's Inn Passage. Then it was that Charlie opened his heart.

"Hm!" he grunted. "Pity. Awful pity. Seemed the right thing to do. But it wasn't, Phyl. It was wrong. It was wrong. It was wicked. You can say what you like, but it was a crime, Phyl, and I'm a criminal."

"Oh, rubbish, Charlie!" said I. "What else could you do?"

"What else!" he demanded fiercely.

"Why anything else than what I did. Just think of it. Only three of those beggars and I'd actually got eight cartridges left in the magazine. Oh, wicked, wicked waste!"

"Yes," I agreed, "it does seem rather a pity when you come to think of it."

FLIGHT SIX

Storm and Sunshine

I have remarked – more than once, I think – that I have been the victim of circumstances. And I now repeat the statement. Not, you understand, that I wish to escape from the responsibility for such unconsidered actions as led me into difficulties, but that I don't want to take more than my fair share of the blame for what actually did happen. You'll see what I mean presently.

Now, that last adventure of mine had given my nerves an awful shake-up, as you may imagine. For I had escaped from those horrid kidnapping wretches, with Charlie's help, only by the skin of my teeth; and the worst of it was that, owing to our hurry to get away, and to the darkness and the runaway horse, we neither of us had the faintest idea as to where the brutes lived. So it was of no use to try to set the police on them. Consequently, with the knowledge that those wretches were still at large, and probably lying in wait for me, I hardly dared to show my nose out of doors. In the broadest of broad daylight, I sneaked out to do my shopping and sneaked back to my little flat as quickly as I could, to spend the remainder of a dreary day in novel-reading, needle-work and good resolutions.

The existence of a bachelor girl was apparently not all beer and skittles. It was all very well to have no one to consider but oneself, but it wasn't so agreeable to find the rest of the human race similarly engaged. I daresay married women have their troubles, but, all the same, if there had happened to be in London an establishment like those delightful shops in the Seven Dials where you may see all sorts and conditions of dogs sitting glumly in cages waiting to be bought; if, I say, there had been a similar establishment in which a few cagefuls of eligible husbands were exposed for sale, I think I would have invested in one — always assuming that the proprietor had the right sort of article in stock. But there wasn't such a place, so there was no use in thinking about it.

Meanwhile, I had let myself in for that set of chambers next door — Mr Philip Rowden's. Of course, the mythical Philip Rowden was dead. All that nonsense was at an end. No more masquerading in men's clothes for me, thank you. Still there the rooms were, and they had to be kept tidy; so, by way of finding myself something to do, I climbed up through the trap in my bedroom ceiling, crept along the loft and dropped down into the rooms next door. And thereupon, behold Circumstance popping in through the letter-box, and I suppose if there had been no letter-box, he would have come in through the keyhole.

There were four letters in the box. Three of them looked commercial and turned out to be from moneylenders. But the fourth struck a different note. Its address — in a sort of decorative, neo-gothic lettering written with a broadish pen — set my heart in quite a little flutter. No professional envelope-addresser's hand this, I decided, and my prophetic soul was right, for, when I opened it and glanced at the signature, the bold, comely characters spelled out the name of Paul Everard.

"My dear Rowden," the letter ran, "As the mountain won't come to Mahomet, Mahomet is coming to the mountain — on Tuesday evening, at seven. I have to go to the Borough and am taking you on my way. If you won't be in stick a card outside your door."

Here was a pretty pickle! Of course, there was no escape, though for me to receive a man alone in these chambers was sailing pretty near the wind. Still, it had to be. I couldn't be uncivil to him after the great service he had rendered me. And then he was such a dear! If only there had been a shop of the kind I have described, and I could have seen him sitting outside in a nice little cage – but what nonsense I am talking! Well, the long and the short of it was that I had to receive him, and as this was Tuesday, there was no time to lose in making the necessary preparations.

Now, how do men entertain one another? That was the problem that faced me. I had a vague idea that, when alone together, they usually drank whisky and smoked. Probably, they also talked about women, but this was a mere surmise based upon an obvious analogy. The whisky, with its natural accompaniment of soda-water, and the tobacco were the elements of certainty and must be procured without delay, for I must make as masculine an appearance as possible to cover any "howlers" in the matter of male etiquette into which my ignorance might precipitate me.

But you've no idea what a lot of trouble that whisky gave me. It was my absurd self-consciousness, you know. Instead of simply going to the grocer like a sensible person, I must needs go prowling up and down Fleet Street in search of a quiet shop where I could make my purchase unobserved, and naturally failed to find one. For a few seconds I halted irresolutely outside the emporium of a certain Mr Mooney, until a flat-faced dipsomaniac in the doorway with a green necktie and three-quarters of a yard of upper lip, raised his hat and winked, which obviously made Mooney's establishment impossible. At last I found a sedate little wine shop with a nice motherly-looking woman behind the counter and agreeably free from customers; but even there I stole in with the air of a female Guy Fawkes, and, as I leaned confidentially across the counter and asked, almost in a whisper, for a bottle of whisky, I felt myself turning the colour of a tomato.

The woman looked at me in pained surprise and asked sadly whether I would have Scotch or Irish. Of course, I didn't care a dump, but sheer revulsion from the offensive Mooney made me say, "Scotch, please," whereupon the woman fished up a bottle from some hidden receptacle and began gloomily to swathe it in very soft paper which she moulded to its form with most unnecessary accuracy. She was still so engaged when an elderly clergyman entered the shop and looked inquisitively from the bottle to me and from me back to the bottle, whereupon, of course, I turned redder than ever. And then the idiot of a woman must needs stop to remark: "This whisky has rather a smoky flavour; I don't know whether you object to that."

"It isn't for myself," I replied, nearly crying with embarrassment, as the parson cast a shocked glance at me and then looked away.

"The smoky taste," the old imbecile continued, "is due to the peat – at least so I'm told. People who like the flavour consider it rather pleasant, but those who don't like it consider it quite disagreeable. Of course, if you're used to it – "

"It isn't for my own use," I explained once more.

"No," the old driveller agreed. "Well, I thought I'd mention it because, if you don't happen to like the flavour you may find it a little unpleasant, though, of course, when you get used to it – "

"I really don't care what it tastes like," I said. "I'm not going to drink it."

"No," rejoined the old natural. "Exactly. But I thought I'd better mention it because, although it's only the peat smoke – at least that's what I'm told – "

Here my patience suddenly gave out. Snatching up the bottle and tucking it under my arm, I slapped five half-crowns on the counter and stared at them stonily until they were gathered up and replaced by a sixpence, when I stalked majestically out of the shop. It had been a disconcerting interview and my self-possession was still below zero when I wandered vaguely into a tobacconist's and then suddenly realized that I didn't know what to ask for. I really wanted cigars. But what sort of cigars? Of course, I could have asked, but where is the woman who is capable of admitting that she doesn't know?

"Yes," said the sour-looking curmudgeon behind the counter, fixing a speculative eye on the bottle under my arm.

"Oh, I want a box of cigarettes, please. Egyptians." (I knew all about Egyptian cigarettes because a girl friend of mine used to smoke them.)

"Fifty or a hundred?" demanded the curmudgeon, with his eyes still glued to my bottle.

"A hundred," I replied, from sheer nervousness.

He clawed a box down from a shelf, and, slapping it on a sheet of paper, began to wrap it up, mumbling audibly.

"Pretty pass the world's coming to! With their cigarettes and their whiskies and sodas. Hm! Like to see a daughter of mine at it. I'd whisky her. Fetch her a clip over the ear, that's what I'd do. There you are, eight shillings."

He thrust the box at me ungraciously, and having dropped the change for my sovereign into a little glass saucer, glared at me as I picked it up and retired, indignant but crestfallen. He was really a most horrid old man.

And now you see how circumstances trampled on all my good resolutions. By half-past six I had put aside my wig, combed my short hair, dressed myself in one of Charlie's spare suits and, in short, resurrected the mythical Philip Rowden from the oblivion to which I had so lately consigned him. A few minutes later, that pernicious counterfeit, having been duly conveyed, via the bedroom ceiling and the loft into his "dread abode" next door, might have been seen there sprawling in a brand-new armchair by a brand-new occasional table on which reposed a bottle of whisky, a siphon of soda-water and a box of cigarettes – all brand-new and intact. But, my word! What a twitter I was in! goodness knows why. It may have been the brazen impudence of the whole thing and the fear of being bowled out – or it may not. All I know is that as seven o'clock approached I developed something very like St. Vitus' Dance, and when, almost as St Dunstan's clock struck the hour, there came a loud rapping on my oak, I shot out of my chair like a mechanical frog and tottered to the door in a state of gelatinous tremor.

It *was* Paul — Mr Everard, I mean, of course. That was a relief, though somehow the sight of his tall figure on the threshold only made my heart thump the more boisterously. However, when his big muscular hand closed on mine, mere psychical disturbances were instantly obscured by physical agony. I could have screamed. Why *do* men squash one another's hands in this ridiculous way?

"Well, old man," said he, "so I've run you to earth at last. You're an unsociable young devil, never to come and look me up. Why haven't you?"

I mumbled some vague excuses as I furtively chafed my fingers, and, having offered him a chair, pushed the cigarette box and the bottle towards him.

"Have some whisky," said I.

He shook his head. "No thanks, old chap," he replied, "but I'll smoke a pipe, if you don't object to the smell of shag."

The apologetic tone rather disconcerted me. Why should I object? Do men generally? Moreover, as he sat filling a vicious-looking black pipe, those strange, dark blue eyes of his strayed about the room with an expression of intelligent curiosity that made my flesh creep. He was obviously "taking notice," as the nurses say. But what was he noticing? Could it be that my household gods were playing me false and giving away my little fraud? I watched him anxiously, not a little distracted by my growing admiration of his splendid manhood. For really, as he lolled with easy grace in the little arm-chair, he looked a perfectly superb creature massive and powerful as a Hercules and yet as supple as a cat; and his face, too, so alert, so masterful and daring, and yet so earnest and thoughtful, with something dreamy and tender in those wonderful blue eyes that were wandering enquiringly about the room, and had now settled with an amused twinkle on the untouched whisky bottle and the unrifled cigarette box. And at this moment he raised them and looked full into mine, and instantly I felt the blood rush into my cheeks.

"You're a rum chap, Rowden," said he. "I'm glad I knew you before I saw your diggings."

"Why?" I asked in blank dismay.

"Because," he replied, "I should have misjudged you. Why, my dear fellow, this is like a girl's room. Look at those window curtains and those fal-de-lals on the wall and all this pretty furniture! If I hadn't known what a spunky young beggar you can be at a pinch, I should have taken you for a regular Mary Ann."

"I'm sorry you don't like my rooms," I said sulkily.

"I didn't say so. 'The foxes have holes and the birds of the air have nests.' Everyone to his taste. These rooms wouldn't fit me. I should feel as big a fool as a fox sitting in a sparrow's nest. But they suit you to a t, and I like them for that reason and because I like you, old chap. And I'm glad to see that you don't drink whisky or smoke cigarettes."

I was on the point of asking him how he knew, but that would have been a silly question. It did not require the powers of a Sherlock Holmes to reach that conclusion.

We chatted for some time, principally about the old Inn – which seemed to have taken his fancy amazingly – and the Temple and Staple Inn and the various other survivals from the more picturesque London of the past. Presently he looked at his watch.

"I can't stay very long this time, Rowden," said he, "because I've got a job to do for a chum of mine. He has started a little pottery down in Lambeth – in that building, in fact, from which I saw you scuffling with those brigands. Well, he is having a one-man show of his stuff up west, and, as he happens to be laid up just at present, I am going down to his place to see the things packed and sent off. So I must hook it in a few minutes. By the way, I suppose you wouldn't care to come with me? I should be awfully glad if you would. I could do with some help and I should like you to see the stuff. There's nothing else like it made in this country. What do you say?"

I didn't know what to say. I wanted, most frightfully, to go. But, on the other hand, I was in a regular ultramarine funk of being out at night alone. Of course, as long as I was with Paul – Mr Everard, I mean; I can *not* keep the proprieties in mind – I had no fear whatever. But I couldn't very well ask him to see me home without standing confessed an unmitigated Mary Ann.

I cogitated profoundly – and rapidly, and with the result that is inevitable in the case of an intelligent female.

"I'll tell you what, Mr Everard," said I, "I'll come and help you to pack your crockery if you'll have supper with me afterwards at some nice little restaurant and then come back here for a pipe and a chat."

"Done!" said he. "But for the Lord's sake don't call me Mr Everard. I'm going to call you Phil – you said your name was Philip. I'm Paul Everard. You can use which name you like, but drop the Mister in any case. And, with regard to this supper question, couldn't we pick up a bit of grub on the way home and eat it here? It would be a lot cheaper and I don't mind telling you that I'm on the save; have to be, you know."

I agreed instantly. I had meant him to be my guest, of course, but I couldn't say so after he had said that he was in low water. Besides it would be ever so much more cosy to sup together alone and so delightfully improper, too! So that was settled, and a few minutes later I fetched a hat and stick of Charlie's from the bedroom – where I had fortunately planted them for the sake of appearances – and, having made sure that I had my latch-key, I set forth with Paul – as I now have his permission to call him – in my new adventure.

How delightful it was to be out in the streets once more, swinging along fearlessly by the side of my unconscious champion! Rapidly my spirits rose and bubbled over in a stream of gleeful babblings, to which my big friend listened with appreciative smiles, glancing at me from time to time with the sort of fond amusement with which one views the gambols of a puppy or a kitten.

"You're a cheerful young rip, Phil," he remarked with a chuckle, and then he added, just a little wistfully, I thought, "It's a blessed thing to be happy, blessed for everyone, I mean, for happiness radiates out like the warmth of a fire and makes other people happy. Go on, Phil. Babble some more."

Of course I refused indignantly. I hadn't come out to play the part of a gas stove or a hot water pipe, and I told him so. At which he chuckled again, and so started me chattering afresh. Presently, however, he gave me a little information. It seemed that a friend of his had met Charlie and had heard the story of our great adventure, which he had duly passed on to Paul, who related it to me.

"It's rather a mysterious affair," he concluded. "It seems that this dago scoundrel has some sort of grudge against Sidley – which, by the way, solves another mystery that has puzzled me a good deal; I mean, why those brigands were trying to get hold of you when I came to your assistance. Evidently they were some of the same gang and had mistaken you for Sidley, and as they may make the same mistake again, I should advise you to be careful where you go, especially at night."

"You can trust me for that," said I; "but I'm not so sure about Charlie."

"Neither am I," said Paul, "though he's a cool-headed chap in spite of his rashness. But it's poor Miss Dudley that I'm most troubled about. That dago beast will do all he knows now to get hold of her, if only for the sake of revenge; and the Lord help her if he does! My aunt! but I'd like to have an interview with that gentleman! He wouldn't get off with a black eye, or even two. I'd make it a permanent cure, if I went to chokee for it. Here we are. This is our show."

He halted before a large, black-painted door in an otherwise blank wall, and, inserting a key, opened it and entered. When he had lit the gas I saw that we were in a small office, from which we passed out into what was evidently the principal workshop; a great, bare place, furnished with a couple of fire-clay furnaces, a potter's wheel and a lathe, with a small gas engine to drive them, a number of galvanized iron bins and, at one side on a long bench, the collection of pottery that we had come to pack. We went over to the bench together to look at the exhibits, and Paul expounded their beauty to me, with a great deal of enthusiasm and, as it seemed to me. a considerable amount of knowledge; so much so, in fact, that for the first time it occurred to me to wonder what he was by profession.

But his enthusiasm was not unjustified. They were a singularly beautiful lot of pieces, ranging from simple vases and bowls to statuettes and busts, something like the old Bow and Chelsea figures, but quieter in colour and more simply and broadly treated.

"Well, Phil," said Paul, when we had looked over the whole collection; "how do you like them?"

"They're jolly," I answered, "all of them, but especially the figures. And what a delightful little bust that is. Do you suppose it's a portrait or just an imaginary head?"

He looked at the bust speculatively for a while, and then turned to me with the queerest expression that you can imagine.

"Imaginary, I suppose," said he, "though, really, Phil, it's not so very unlike what you'd be if you were a girl. And a ripping fine girl you'd make, let me tell you."

"Thanks," said I, "you're very flattering, but I think I can do all right as a man. Still, I'll consider your suggestion."

"Do, old man," he chuckled, and, as the bell rang at this moment he added: "There are the carriers. I'll go and let them in, and then we shall have to get the things packed."

There wasn't much packing to do, after all, for the carrier's men had brought cases and quantities of wrapping paper, and, as they were regular "fine art carriers," they knew more about it than we did. All that we had to do was to look on and follow each case out to the van as if we had been chief mourners. We had just seen the last but one deposited when a bushy-bearded man in an apron accosted Paul. I didn't hear what he said, as I went back to see the last case packed, but when he came in he said:

"That fellow tells me that there are some cases which he thinks belong to my friend Sharpe, lying in a warehouse on Blue Lion Wharf. He wants me to go down and see if they are Sharpe's, and, if so, to say what is to be done with them. So, when we've finished, we had better pop round there, and then it will be Ho! for the pork-pie shop and Clifford's Inn."

As the last case was carried away he turned out the gas and we followed the bearers out to the van. We saw the cases stowed and the tail-board fastened up, and then, as the van drove away, Paul locked the door, pocketed the key, and, linking his arm in mine, strode away briskly down the street.

It was not far to Blue Lion Wharf. When we got there we found the wicket in the gate open and the bearded man waiting just inside. He shut and bolted the wicket after us, and then walked on ahead of us down a short passage, from which we emerged on to the wharf opposite a flight of slimy-looking stone steps that led down to the water. Passing the steps, we entered an alley between two rows of windowless buildings, near the end of which our conductor halted opposite an open door. On the threshold stood a lighted candle lantern – for the dusk was closing in and the interior of the warehouse was as dark as a vault.

"The cases are in there," said the bearded man, "down at the further end. You'd better take the lantern so as you can read the addresses."

Paul picked up the lantern and entered the warehouse, and I was about to follow when the man elbowed me aside, and, quickly closing the door, turned the great key that projected from the massive lock. With a cry of alarm I darted forward to seize the key, but in a moment the wretch had grasped my arm and pushed me backwards. I shouted again for help and made a frantic grab at the man's beard, which instantly came away in my hand, exposing the shaven and well-remembered face of the villain Isaacs, who had driven the cab in which I had last been spirited away.

As my eyes lighted on that loathsome face, I uttered a shriek of terror, which was cut short by a hand that was clapped over my mouth from behind. At the same moment an invisible hand gripped my free arm, and, pressing it against my body, held me quite powerless. And then O! Heavens! I shudder, even now, as I write it! – the foreign wretch – the dago – stepped quietly from behind me and stood looking into my face with a smile of devilish satisfaction. He held a coil of thin rope in his plump, womanish hands, and this he now began to pass around my arms just above the elbows, securing it finally with a knot at the back.

"It is my beautiful young friend," he murmured in a soft, horrible, caressing tone. "But what have you done with your hair, my pretty one? You have cut off those lovely tresses! Ah! But what a pity! What a pity! And your good brother, he seems impatient."

This last remark, of course, referred to Paul, who was kicking furiously at the door, though, poor fellow! he might as well have kicked at Plymouth Breakwater.

" 'Tain't 'er brother," said Isaacs. "I reckon it's 'er fancy man. Big cove. Looks a tough card, too."

The dago villain gave a scowl of disappointed malice.

"I wanted the brother," he said, viciously.

"Well, yer won't git 'im," said Isaacs, "unless yer wait for another ship. We 'ad all our work cut out for to cop this young woman."

"You are fools," growled the foreign demon, "you should have caught the brother. But, as you have not, put on the gag and secure her in the shed. Then go as fast as you can and fetch the boat."

Once again I experienced the horrible sensation of having my mouth covered by a disgusting pad, which was adjusted and fixed in place by the brute behind me. Then I was hustled into a shed opposite to the one in which Paul was imprisoned and fastened by a turn of rope to one of the posts that supported the roof.

"Now go for the boat, and go quickly," said the archdemon, and the two ruffians — of whom I now recognized the second as the man Jacob, who had captured me last time — hurried out of the shed and disappeared.

My captor stood before me with his hands in his pockets and for a while gloated over his success in silence. I could see little but his silhouette against the open doorway, though the dusk of the summer evening was closing in very gradually and it was still by no means dark outside, but I could fill in the details from the view I had had of him in the open. His buff dust coat, his ridiculous, gaudy waistcoat with its pattern of silken flowers, his jewelled tie-pin, massive watch-chain and the multitudinous rings on his plump, white fingers – I could see them all in the dusky shape that stood between me and the open doorway, in spite of the darkness. Though, to be sure, my glance travelled constantly past that hated form to the door of Paul's prison which was visible through the opening.

"I am sorry not to meet your charming brother," the archfiend remarked at length. "I should have liked him to accompany us when we start tonight on our voyage to the beautiful western lands." He took his fat hands out of his pockets to rub them together, and, as he paused, I felt myself almost fainting with the horror and sickening fear that his last words had aroused. Tonight! I was to be carried on board some ship manned, evidently, by a crew of ruffians in this wretch's pay. Then, it seemed that all hope was at an end, and it remained only to consider whether I could perchance contrive to fling myself into the water and find safety in death before I reached that floating inferno.

"I am sorry for your friend, too," the villain resumed, "because we shall have to leave him behind. But he will not be lonely," he continued, with a horrible, soft chuckle. "There are many rats in this place. And he seems to be a wise man, this friend of yours. You notice he has now grown quite patient. He no longer makes those foolish noises."

This was true. For some time past, the furious kicking at the door had ceased, and the only sounds that issued from Paul's prison were occasional, obscure noises, as if the captive were groping among the lumber in search of some opening or means of escape. And presently even these sounds ceased and were succeeded by a stillness that seemed like the very silence of despair.

But suddenly that silence was rent by a thunderous crash. The door split and the fragments flew outwards, followed by two great masses of timber, a barrel of solidified cement – and Paul, armed with a ponderous spar – apparently a boat's mast – and looking like an avenging fury.

At the crash and the bursting open of the door, the foreign wretch uttered a shrill scream and darted out of the shed in the direction of the gate. In that direction, too, Paul disappeared, and at a similar pace, as I could judge by the quick patter of the two sets of footsteps. I listened with eager anxiety as they rapidly faded away, and when I could hear them no more, I still listened, trembling with fear mingled with faintly reviving hope and wondering what was taking place out there on the quay. I was not left long in suspense. In quite a short time I caught the sound of returning footsteps – a firm, rhythmical tread that my heart instantly recognized – and in a few moments Paul appeared at the opening with the great pole over his shoulder.

It is a mercy that I was tied up to that post. If I had not been, I should certainly have flung myself on his breast and burst into tears of gratitude and joy, and so given myself away irretrievably. But that post, and his first words, saved me, for, as he came opposite the doorway, he peered in and sang out in a cheery voice that instantly brought me to my senses:

"Are you in there, Phil, old man?"

Naturally I wasn't able to answer excepting by making a series of obscure snorts through my nose. But these inarticulate sounds conveyed my meaning sufficiently, for he immediately rested the pole against the lintel of the doorway and came in, striking a wax match.

"The damned scoundrels!" he muttered as the light of the match revealed my condition. "Keep still, old chap, while I cut this cord."

A sweep of his pocket knife released me from the post, and another set my hands free, and, as we came out of the doorway a third cut let the filthy gag drop from my mouth.

"Where is he?" I gasped, as soon as my mouth was uncovered.

"Oh, he's gone, and I fancy he won't come back. But where are those other two devils – there were two, weren't there?"

"Yes. They've gone to fetch a boat."

"I see. Well, I think I'll stay and have a few words with them, but, meanwhile, you just walk up the alley and wait for me by the gate. And if you see them coming your way, you nip outside and make yourself scarce and sing out for help."

"You'd much better not wait for them," I said coaxingly. "Let us go away together while the coast is clear."

He turned on me fiercely. "Now, look here, Phil," he said, in a stern voice, "you do as I tell you. D'you hear?"

I heard, and a glance at his face compelled unquestioning obedience. There was no dreamy tenderness in it now. Every line and feature spoke of grim purpose and iron resolution.

He shouldered his pole and we set forward together down the alley between the warehouses and across the wharf. In the twilight I could see the dark water brimming up nearly to the edge of the quay and lipping over the slippery stone steps. But he hurried me by in silence, and it was only when we reached the end of the passage that he spoke again.

"Now, Phil," said he, "you cut along up to the gate and unbolt it, and wait there for me, unless you see either of those devils, in which case you just pop out and run for it until you see a bobby. So long, old chap."

I would have protested again, but dared not. There was nothing for it but to obey. With infinite reluctance I took my way up the passage towards the gate, only stopping once to look back as the passage made a sharp turn. In the dim light I could see him standing near the steps, but hidden from them by an angle of the wall; and it seemed to me, as he stood there so still and watchful, resting his pole on the ground as if it had been a spear or pike, while he gazed out across the darkening river, that he looked like some Roman sentinel awaiting with grim composure the attack of a stealthy foe.

I waited in the passage just inside the gate listening anxiously for his footsteps until quite a long time had passed. Then I went back a little way and listened more intently. But still he did not come. My uneasiness grew into alarm and then into positive terror.

What could he be doing? Those two men were, as I well knew, unscrupulous wretches, and he was all alone. Supposing anything should have happened to him – should be happening at this very moment!

At last, unable to bear the suspense any longer I walked warily but quickly down the passage until I came out on the wharf. And then I breathed again, for there he was, safe and sound, tidily stowing the pole by the wall of a shed, and, to my surprise, quite alone.

"Haven't they come yet?" I asked.

"Oh, yes," he replied, "and gone away again."

I looked out over the dim river, but there was no boat in sight – excepting one that was floating bottom upwards on the tide close inshore, and they certainly couldn't be in that. But the darkness was closing in now, and they might easily have pulled out of sight. I looked at Paul, as he came up and linked his arm in mine, and noticed that the stem expression had given place to one of quiet satisfaction.

"Now, my hearty," said he, "let us be off and set a course for the pie-shop. I hope you are hungry."

I wasn't a bit. What I really wanted was to have a good cry to settle my nerves, but, of course, that was out of the question. So I expressed a deep interest in the pie, and we set forth together in search of it.

"Don't you think," I said, as we were striding across Blackfriars Bridge, "that we had better drop in at a police station and tell them about those wretches? They could be traced now through the wharf people, you know."

He shook his head decidedly. "No," said he. "It isn't necessary. You can take it from me that they won't give us any more trouble. And the less said about this little affair the better."

I was rather puzzled as to how he could be so sure that they would give us no more trouble, but it did not occur to me to doubt him. So I dismissed the subject from my mind, and a great relief it was.

We bought a veal and ham pie in Fleet Street, and Paul insisted on wasting his substance by buying a bottle of claret, which he would pay for as well as the pie. And I bought some nice little custardy things with paper frills round them, which I had to carry most awfully carefully, and so we came home to the dear old Inn – which I had never hoped to see again – going in through the gate by St Dunstan's Church.

My goodness! what a feast we had! There wasn't much style about it, because as I had forgotten to bring any plates across from my rooms, we had to eat off the paper bags and cut the pie with Paul's pocket knife. But that only made it the more jolly. And when I had had half a tumbler of claret I was so elated that I could have cried for joy, but, as that was not permissible, I babbled unceasingly until Paul fairly shouted with laughter.

It *was* a time! When Paul went away, about half-past eleven – after having exacted a promise from me to return his visit – he left me in a dream of bliss. For we were real friends now, and the haunting terror of those kidnapping wretches was lifted from me for ever.

There is a little sequel which I must just mention, though it really has nothing to do with my story. But it is such a queer coincidence that it seems worth while to note it in passing. About a week after my adventure, when I was looking over the paper, I happened to come on the report of an inquest on the body of a man who was found in the river. It was really awfully queer. The body was dressed in a buff dust coat and a silk flowered waistcoat, and it had a jewelled tie-pin and a number of valuable rings on the fingers; in fact the description was so like that of the foreign wretch that if I hadn't known that he was on the way to South America I should have supposed that he must have tumbled into the river.

But there are a lot of curious coincidences in life as I daresay you have noticed.

FLIGHT SEVEN

Love and a Graven Image

If I hadn't already remarked on several occasions that I have been the victim of circumstances, I should be disposed to make the remark now. But you can't go on saying the same thing over and over again, even if it's true, and, after all, on serious consideration, I am not so absolutely sure that it is. As to the circumstances, I am quite clear; I stick to them like cobbler's wax. But when I speak of myself as a victim – well, perhaps I had better leave you to judge, and in the meantime I'll get back to the circumstances.

You may remember that when I said "goodbye" to Paul Everard on that eventful and delicious evening when he supped with me at my chambers, I promised to return his visit. Strictly speaking, I suppose I ought not to have made any such promise. But I did, and you can't go back on a definite promise – especially if you don't want to.

Still, it would be sailing uncommonly near the wind. It had been bad enough for me to receive a young man all alone in my chambers, though I hadn't invited him, but to visit him at his own rooms, in cold blood – at least, not in such very cold blood, but of my own free will – was really most improper. And yet I couldn't escape from that promise, and I didn't mean to.

It was a complicated situation. As to Paul, it was perfectly simple, as simple as he was himself. He supposed that I was a young man. Never dreamed of anything different. He had jumped to this ridiculous conclusion for no better reason than that, whenever he had met me, I had had my hair cut short and was wearing a suit of Charlie's clothes. But isn't that just like a man? And doesn't it make one wonder what would become of the poor dears if there were no women to look after them and protect them?

However, as I say, it was a complicated situation. As Mr Philip Rowden I was bound to keep my engagement; as Miss Phyllis Dudley, I had no business ever to have had any engagement to keep. You see my dilemma. The two halves of my dual personality had conflicting duties, and, of course, you see, as I did, that the one who could not possibly escape was Mr Philip Rowden.

I did not embark on that visit to Paul without consideration. By no means. For days and days I thought of nothing else. I took the smartest of Charlie's suits to the tailor's and had it cleaned and ironed. I bought a new hat and gloves and a smart little walking-stick, and, as my hair was getting a little long at the back, I went to a barber's and had it cut. I worried the man so much with directions as to how I wanted it to be trimmed that he grew quite impatient, and at last insisted on shaving me which was a most horrid experience and made me feel devoutly thankful that Nature has exempted the female countenance from the curse of whiskers.

The dusk was just closing in as I set forth from my chambers on my latest adventure, figged out in Charlie's smart suit, with my new hat, gloves, and walking-stick, as spruce as the frog in the children's song. Only I wasn't going a-wooing, you understand. I was just going to make a friendly call. Well, I crept down the stairs and out of the entry, and was just going to dart out through the postern gate into Fetter Lane when I observed Mr Larkin, the porter, standing there talking to one of the residents. Instantly, I turned and headed for Clifford's Inn Passage, but he had seen me, and I could hear him pattering after me bleating:

"Mr Sidley! One moment, sir! Can I have a word – "

Here I popped round the corner through the archway, and collided heavily with a stout woman who was carrying a number of cardboard boxes. They might have been kettledrums from the noise they made on the flagged floor of the passage, and as for the woman herself, the phillaloo she raised was perfectly ridiculous, especially when Mr Larkin came flying round the corner and trod on one of the boxes – as I gathered from her remarks. At the end of the passage I saw an empty taxi crawling eastward. The driver caught my eye and slowed down further; I wrenched the door open, and, yelling out "Mark Lane" tumbled in and slammed the door. I hadn't the least idea where Mark Lane was, and, of course, I didn't want to go there, but I had to say something, and that was the first name that occurred to me. However, when my nerves had settled down a little, by which time we had reached Ludgate Hill, I decided that I wasn't going to be taken all over London just because Mr Larkin had mistaken me for Charlie, so I stopped the cab and said to the driver:

"I think Hampstead Road would be nearer where I want to go."

"But," expostulated the driver, "Hampstead Road ain't nowhere near Mark Lane."

"No," I replied, "I know. That's what I mean. Hampstead Road, corner of George Street."

The driver turned round on his seat and stared in at me as if I had been some queer sort of animal in a cage. It was quite embarrassing. Goodness knows how long he would have sat there staring at me if he had been left to himself, but, fortunately, a policeman intervened and sent him off with a flea in his ear, to my great relief, and away we went up St Andrew's Hill. But he evidently thought that there was something queer about me, for, when I got out at the corner of George Street, he fixed me with a look of such devouring curiosity that I took the first opportunity to bolt down a side street and get out of sight.

I didn't go straight to Jacob Street, but approached it strategically in a somewhat zig-zag and serpentine fashion. The fact is, and I don't mind admitting it, that I was as nervous as a cat. It wasn't merely the impropriety of the whole affair or the complications that loomed in the future. It was Paul himself. He was something entirely new in my experience. The ordinary man I viewed with that indulgent pity that is natural to the human female in respect – or, perhaps, I should say, in disrespect – of the male. But Paul was different. His impressive personality dominated me completely. I positively stood in awe of him, I did indeed. Which was a new sensation for me.

And, after all, it wasn't only awe that made me approach the vicinity of Jacob Street with my heart in my mouth. I may as well confess, especially as you have probably guessed already, that I was a good deal – what shall I say? Oh! you needn't snigger. It was perfectly natural if you remember the risks that he had taken for me. And it's all very well to say that good looks lie only on the surface. Who cares? He wasn't going to turn himself inside out. So the surface was good enough for me.

My strategic approach landed me at last, very tremulous and excited, on the threshold of the wide, factory-like door of number 63, and, as I pulled the bell handle above the little brass plate inscribed "Mr Everard," I speculated once more on the avocation of my mysterious friend. What did he do behind that wide door? Was he a manufacturer of some kind? Did he make boots or pickles or some other sort of unromantic but useful commodities? It was possible, and yet it was difficult to associate those dreamy, compelling, dark blue eyes with say, jam or boot-polish. Still, he had to live, and, of course – but at this point a wicket in the door opened and Paul himself appeared in the half light within. His appearance struck me with something like dismay. He wore a coarse linen blouse, of which the wrists were turned up, and a long apron of the same material, on which he wiped his hands as he recognized me. It was not a becoming costume, and I found the suggestion of manual labour that it conveyed by no means agreeable. "Every woman," says the poet, "is a rake at heart." If he had said "a snob" he would have been nearer the mark.

"Why, Phil, my dear boy," exclaimed Paul, holding out the wiped hand, "this is an unexpected pleasure. I began to think that you were never coming to see me."

"I hope I'm not disturbing you," I said, as he drew me through the wicket into a wide dimly-lighted hall or passage.

"By Jove! but you are," he replied, "and mighty glad I am to be disturbed. I've done enough work for today. Do you mind if I run out and get some tobacco before we settle down for a yarn?"

"Of course I don't."

"Then I'll scoot. You'll find the door of the workshop at the bottom of the yard, and be careful that you don't fall over those blocks of stone that are lying about down there. And you might take my apron. I shan't be more than a minute or two."

He unfastened the apron, and, handing it to me, took a dusty felt hat from a peg and went out. I watched him through the wicket as he strode down the street, apparently quite indifferent to the figure that he cut, and, for the millionth time, I found myself marvelling at the incomprehensible oddities of the human male. I wouldn't have walked down the street in that blouse and that battered old hat for a thousand pounds.

A little chilled by this unconventional reception, and wondering what industrial disillusionment awaited me at the bottom of the yard, I took my way down the flagged path, casting an inquisitive eye on a stack of thin stone slabs that were reared against a wall and a number of large white blocks that flanked the path and that looked like enormous lumps of loaf sugar. At the bottom of the yard was a detached building with a wide double door and a wicket like that through which I had just come, and, as this stood ajar, I pushed it open and entered.

At first, I found myself in almost total darkness, but, stretching out my hand, I felt a thick curtain, which I drew aside; and then I got one of the greatest surprises of my life. The interior of the building formed a single vast chamber or hall, lighted by one enormous window and a skylight screened with blinds. On the white-washed walls and the front of a sort of musicians' gallery that ran along one end, hung a multitude of plaster casts, trusses, brackets, masks, reliefs, door-heads, mantels, mural monuments and all sorts of ornamental details. A large row of galvanized iron bins, like those that I had seen at the Lambeth factory, were ranged along one side, and on the other were a number of rough wooden pedestals which supported plaster heads, busts or statuettes, and three or four massive easels – each shrouded in a large sheet of American cloth – occupied part of the floor space. This was what I saw in the single, instantaneous glance that I cast around the great, barn-like interior; but it was only a single glance; for my eyes lighted on an object that rose from the centre of the floor, and when I had seen that, I had no eyes for anything else.

Let me try to describe it as well as I can. The figure of a woman, somewhat above life size, youthful but grave and majestic, tender and gracious yet resolute and strong, lightly and gracefully poised upon a globe supported by smaller globes, the arms partly extended, the hands upraised in unison with the slightly upturned face. It was exquisitely treated. Dignified, reticent, restrained, with no trace of extravagance in pose or gesture, the allegory yet spoke its meaning to the first glance. Aspiration – a noble yearning – was expressed in every line and in every movement, and so lightly was the figure poised upon the bubble-like globe that it seemed to be without weight, and looked as if it might at any moment soar away from its resting place. The very draperies expressed the same conception, for they seemed to float by their own buoyancy rather than merely to hang.

I stood before the statue in a trance of amazement and admiration. Even the disfiguring framework of iron bars and struts that supported the ponderous mass of clay, and the ugly revolving platform on which it was reared, failed to detract from its beauty. One could forget them in looking at the soft figure that seemed to rise like a thing of life and more than human loveliness, just as one can ignore the rattle of organ pedals or the creak of the swell shutter, if only the music be good enough. And this was a great work of art. I had no doubt of that. Years ago, you will remember,

I had put in some time as an art student at the Slade School, and if I had not profited very greatly by my studies there, I had at least learned to realize the immeasurable gulf that yawns between mere students' work and an actual masterpiece.

And this wonderful thing had been done by Paul! It was his creation! The noble thought and the delightful poetic fancy that breathed from every line of it were his thought and his fancy. It was an amazing reflection. It made me feel quite *emotionée*. But I had to keep myself in hand, for, just then I heard a quick step coming down the paved yard, the door opened and in came Paul, minus the unseemly hat, but plus a newspaper parcel from which the end of a French loaf poked out. He came and stood by my side, looking up at the statue, and after a few moment's silence asked:

"What do you think of her, Phil?"

I turned to him and I suppose something of what I felt must have appeared in my face – indeed, I could have fallen on his neck then and there – for he looked at me a little shyly, and, as I met those wonderful blue eyes, my own filled.

"Paul!" I murmured. "I can't – and to think that you never told me!"

He turned away a little abruptly and began discharging his cargo into a cupboard.

"Didn't know you were interested in effigies, Phil," he replied, thrusting the loaf into the recesses of the cupboard. "May I take it that you approve?"

"Approve!" I exclaimed. "It's the most beautiful thing I have ever seen."

"Oh, come!" he protested, "draw it mild, old chap. Still, I'm glad you like it. It's the best thing I've ever done. You're going to have a bit of grub with me, I hope?"

I accepted cheerfully and he then inducted me into the "Banqueting Hall," a corner of the great studio by the fireplace enclosed by high painted canvas screens and comfortably carpeted with rugs. Here I helped him to lay the supper table, and I noted with pleasure that his Bohemianism was tempered by a certain odd fastidiousness. For though the food was of the simplest – most of it had come from the paper parcel – the table appointments, even to the very cloth, were all what the dealers would call "collector's pieces." When we had set it out, the table had quite a distinguished appearance, with its old Flemish glasses, its Sheffield plate, its pewter and old china, together with the picturesque French loaf and a quarter-flask of Chianti that had been brought out in my honour.

While I was giving the finishing touches to the table he went up to a room that opened off the gallery to wash and change, whence he presently returned looking quite spruce, and, having lowered the gas lights in the studio, came into the "hall" and took his seat at the table. Naturally, as we supped, our talk came back to the statue.

"It's finished, isn't it?" I asked.

"Yes," he replied. "I tinker at it now and again, but it's really finished."

"And are you going to carve it in marble yourself?"

"Not marble," said he. "It isn't suitable. Too much top weight and too slender at the base. I modelled it for bronze."

"Is it a commission?"

"No. Absolutely unprovoked."

"Then what are you going to do with it?"

"Break it up, I suppose, and dump the clay back in the bins."

I looked at him in incredulous horror.

"You don't mean," I exclaimed, "that you are going to destroy that lovely piece of work?"

"I don't want to," he answered gloomily, "but I expect I shall have to sooner or later. You see, Phil, it would cost a mint of money to put it into bronze. Why, the preliminary plaster cast would run me into a matter of fifty pounds, and the founder's bill would be something terrific. Even an electrotype would be quite beyond my means."

I listened with blank dismay. To destroy a finished masterpiece was an absolute crime – a tragedy. It wouldn't bear thinking of.

"I suppose," Paul went on, "you are wondering what the deuce made me do it. I sometimes wonder myself. But artists are unreasonable beasts, Phil. They get an idea into their thick heads and they can't rest until they have given it expression. That's what happened to me. I got the idea of an allegorical figure of Ambition, borne on the Bubble of Hope. It came to me and it stuck. It haunted me. I made a little sketch in wax and rather liked it – I'll show it to you presently. Then I thought I would do a statuette, but the subject was really too big for a statuette. Then I got a rather well-paid job – big stone mantelpiece with supporting figures – and as that put me in funds for the time I made the plunge and started a full-sized figure. It has cost me quite a lot for models, but I have had my value in the pleasure of doing the work. And that's all I'm likely to get out of it. I'd give something to see it in bronze, but you can't have everything you want in this life."

I made no immediate reply, being, in fact, a trifle upset by this pathetic little history. Not that it was a singular one. Its like has been but too often repeated. How many a fine picture has been painted out to save the cost of a new canvas! How many priceless books have died in manuscript and been lost to the world for the lack of a few pounds to pay the printer! Alas! for the tragedy of poverty! But poverty wasn't going to have it all its own way this time. On that point my mind was made up already. And forthwith I put out a delicate feeler.

"Couldn't you borrow enough money to get this figure cast?"

He shook his head impatiently. "I never borrow," he said, curtly. "I don't mind being hard up but I couldn't stand owing money."

"But a friend – " I began.

"Worse still," said he. "I'd sooner hang myself. No, Phil, I'm making a living and I shall shove through in the end."

"By the way, how do you make a living, if it isn't an impertinent question?"

"Mostly by trade work," he replied. "Mantelpieces, tombstones, architects' sculpture, exhibition frames and so on. I modelled those figures that you saw at Sharpe's pottery works."

"Oh indeed! And that little bust that you said was like what I should have been if I had been a girl?"

Paul grinned. "You've got me there, Phil," said he. "So I do borrow from my friends, after all. I ventured to borrow your distinguished mug, as well as I could remember it. Hope you don't mind."

Mind indeed! I felt myself growing pink with pleasure, and so would you if you had been in my place. But, of course I had to say that it was like his cheek.

After supper we browsed round the studio together and Paul showed me the casts of his various "jobs," and a big Celtic cross that he was modelling in clay. Then we enclosed the figure of Ambition in a sort of vapour bath of wet sheeting with an outer tent of oiled linen, and returned to the "hall" where Paul smoked and I conversed until it was time for me to go. I rose reluctantly to make my adieux, for it always seems a pity to put an end to a pleasant episode. However, Paul insisted on walking home with me, which was some consolation, and it was not until we reached the entrance to Clifford's Inn Passage that we actually parted.

It had been a delightful evening. Everything had gone off without a hitch, and the success had made me so confident of Mr Philip Rowden's capabilities that I had freely pledged myself to repeat the visit and meant to keep my promise.

I lay awake quite a long time that night. You see, I had a good deal to think about. There was Paul, for instance. What a splendid fellow he was! The very type of magnificent manhood – but, there, you know what he was like by this time, though you couldn't really appreciate him without having seen him. And when I wasn't thinking of Paul – and sometimes even when I was – that lovely, soft grey figure, the work of his hands, the child of his brain, would rise before me as if appealing to me to save it from annihilation in the clay bins, to preserve it as an undying monument to the genius of its creator. Nor did I intend that the appeal should be in vain. It would have been simply disgraceful of me, with my fat balance at the bank, to let my friend lose the reward of his effort and his inspiration when the calamity could be averted by just selling out a few paltry stocks and shares.

But the question was how to manage it. Clearly a loan was out of the question, for Paul was as proud as Lucifer. And, for the same reason, I felt sure that he would refuse to let me buy the statue after having taken me into his confidence. It was a regular twister. I turned the problem over again and again during the next day or two but never got any farther than a dogged resolution that Paul's masterpiece was to be saved somehow. Perhaps I never should have got any farther if Providence, or Destiny or whatever you call it, hadn't stepped in in conjunction with my cousin Charlie. (By the way, Charlie and Providence – or Destiny – seem to have got a good deal mixed up in my affairs; I hardly know which of them to blame).

It was about noon when the familiar knock came at the door of my chambers. I verified the identity of my visitor through the spy-hole and then opened the door, and in walked my nabs, as cool as a cucumber and as smart as a popinjay. He was inclined to be affectionately demonstrative but I soon put an end to that. I hadn't forgotten Mr Shylock's housemaid, to say nothing of the unknown Winifred and that odious little suffy.

"You're getting beastly starchy all of a sudden, Phyllis," he remarked, sulkily, as he dropped into a chair. "What's the matter? Have I rubbed your fur up the wrong way or has some other fellow taken over the sole performing rights?"

I don't want any of your impudence, Charlie," I replied, rather put out, for I was conscious of having turned as red as a tomato for no reason whatever. His only answer to this was a slow and elaborate wink, and then he sat looking at me and grinning until I could have boxed his ears.

"And what can I do for you?" I asked stiffly. I thought that would have squashed him, but it didn't. He only grinned worse than ever.

"I want you to come and have lunch with me," he replied.

"Do you think I'm going to lunch with a Cheshire cat?" I demanded.

"Of course you are," he chuckled, "at the Cheshire Cheese. Today's Wednesday, beef-steak-pudding day. Have you ever been to the Cheese, Phil?"

Now I never had. I had often wanted to go, but – hadn't quite liked to go alone. So I rather jumped at Charlie's suggestion, his offensive grins notwithstanding. Besides, I was really rather fond of Charlie. He was an awful scallywag but very lovable all the same.

"All right, Phil," said he, in response to my gleeful acceptance. "Then get into your war-paint and come along. I want to have a talk with you about my affairs. But we'll lunch first."

I smiled. Charlie's "affairs" usually resolved themselves into financial problems with no answer, in which the quantities mostly bore the minus sign. Not that he was really a spendthrift or in the least dishonest, but his income was small and he didn't manage it very well. And he never would let me help him, though I was quite well able to afford to.

A few minutes later, we sallied forth together and took our way down Fleet Street to the tavern. It was jolly. I had never been in a London tavern before, and the Cheshire Cheese was so delightfully taverny. You dive up Wine Office Court and you creep in through a sort of dark entry until you find yourself in an ancient, low-ceiled room with a sanded floor and a lot of old fashioned, high-backed settles arranged so as to form little pews with a table in the middle of each. It is awfully nice and homely. And the finishing touches are given by a portrait of that old humbug Dr Johnson, and a little brass plate on the wall showing you the exact spot where he used to rub his greasy old grey wig against the wainscot.

We had hardly taken our places in a pew near the fireplace when a procession came in, bearing a colossal pudding in a stupendous basin, which the bearers set down on a three-legged stool before a sort of high priest in a white cap and clothes and apron to match. I was positively fascinated, and so was everyone else. I sat with my eyes so firmly glued on that enormous pudding that I hardly noticed an elderly gentleman and a girl who had just entered and were standing by the door looking round the room. I say I hardly noticed them; I mean at first. Presently I caught the girl's eye, and then I looked again, and then I looked at the elderly gentleman, and then – Oh, my immortal scissors! as Charlie would say. I wanted to sink through the floor, or creep into the pudding-basin and get under the crust. For the girl was Althea, and the elderly gentleman was none other than Mr John B Potter of New York, U.S.A.

"My eye!" exclaimed Charlie. "What a ripping girl! D'you see her, Phyl? With that old buster near the door. Hallo! They seem to know us, or they think they do."

It was but too true. Althea and her father had simultaneously observed Charlie and were now advancing up the room, beaming with gracious recognition. The fat was in the fire this time and no mistake! What on earth was I to do? I gazed at the advancing couple helplessly and felt my brain congealing with a sort of mental paralysis.

"Who the deuce can they be?" exclaimed Charlie, returning Althea's smile with cent per cent interest. "Don't know 'em from Adam."

Here the couple arrived at our pew, and Mr Potter, flinging out a cordial hand, said heartily: "Well, now, I call this a bit of real luck. We only got back this morning. I haven't even had time to write to you yet. Shan't have to now. Is this your sister, Mr Sidley?"

"No," replied Charlie. "My cousin. Miss Dudley. Let me introduce you."

But he didn't, of course, because he couldn't. He gave a sort of agonized grin and a kind of double-barrelled bow, and I heard him murmur under his breath:

"Who the devil can they be and what's their confounded name?"

However, the grin and the wriggle were accepted in lieu of more formal introduction. Althea and her father shook my hand warmly and the former asked:

"Shall we be disturbing you if we join you at your table?"

"Oh, not in the least," replied Charlie. "We shall be only too delighted."

Accordingly Mr Potter hung up his hat and seated himself opposite me while Althea took the place facing Charles, much to that Scallywag's satisfaction. The former opened the conversation.

"How very remarkably like your cousin you are, Miss Dudley. I have never seen a more extraordinary resemblance. You might be twins."

"So I have been told," I said, cautiously.

"Yes. Most remarkable. And, if you will allow me to say so, Miss Dudley, the resemblance makes you our friend right away. We are very devoted to Mr Sidley. I daresay you know why?"

"No, indeed I don't," I replied. It was an awful fib, but what could I say?"

"He hasn't told you how heroically he saved my daughter's life?"

"No, that he certainly hasn't," I replied, gazing fondly at Charlie, who was pricking up his ears like a terrier at a rabbit-hole. "But," I continued, eagerly grasping at this loop-hole of escape – if you will pardon the rather mixed metaphor – "I should awfully like to hear about it. He never says anything himself. He's so modest."

Charlie grinned rather consciously at this (as well he might), and I could see that he was listening intently, though he kept up a pretence of talking to Althea.

"I'll tell you how it happened," said Mr Potter, "and you shall judge. It was in the Strand near our hotel. My daughter was crossing just in front of a big motor lorry when she slipped and went down full length. The lorry came thundering on and it seemed as if it must go right over her. I gave her up for lost, Miss Dudley, I did indeed. But just then, when the great engine was within a foot or two of her, your cousin darted across, picked my girl up right from under the wheels and had her on the sidewalk in a twinkling. My! but it was a near thing! Before he could get clear, one of the wheels caught him and flung him right across the footway. Another second and he'd have been crushed to atoms. I hope you are none the worse for that fall, Mr Sidley."

"Not in the least, thank you," Charlie replied airily. "I was just a bit bruised and shaken at the time, don't you know. Nothing more."

I heaved a sigh of thankfulness and relief. Good old Charlie! But I might have known that he would be equal to the situation if he only got the ghost of a chance. Now, of course, he knew how things stood, and if I could but make him acquainted with our friend's name, it would be all plain sailing. And it didn't seem a difficult thing to manage, if one watched one's opportunities.

"And so," Mr Potter resumed, "you can understand, Miss Dudley, that I am very devoted to your cousin. I'm his debtor for life. But for him, I'd have lost my daughter, and then I should have lost everything in the world that matters to me, seeing that I am a widower and she's my only child. Your cousin is a very fine young man, Miss Dudley," he added in a lower tone, so as not to abash Charlie too much – but he needn't have been afraid. It takes a good deal to abash Charlie.

"Yes," I murmured in a similarly low tone, "he is, and so modest, too. He has never breathed a word about this. Not a word. He has never even mentioned your name; in fact," I added, as a sort of afterthought, and by way of completing this tissue of falsehoods, "I don't know now what your name is."

"To be sure you don't," he agreed, "but we can easily mend that. My name," (here Charlie paused in the middle of a sentence with his mouth open) "is – what's this. Oh, wine list. What shall we drink? What goes best with beef-steak pudding?"

In my agitation, I suggested sherry and then made it worse by amending in favour of port. Mr Potter chuckled and referred the question to Charlie – as though it mattered a farthing what we drank! – and they had quite a long discussion before they finally settled on Moselle. Then I came back to the really vital question.

"You were saying that your name was – "

"So I was. Yes. My name is – no thank you, waiter, at least not just now. Haven't finished this yet – my name, Miss Dudley, is – but perhaps I'd better give you my card."

He produced from his pocket a fat leather wallet, at which Charlie glared hungrily, and drew from it a card which he pushed across the table to me. I thanked him, and having made a show of reading it, passed it to Charlie, saying: "Would you mind taking care of this for me? I can't get at my pocket just now."

Charlie took it from me with avidity and had a good look at it as he got out his pocket-book. Then, with a sigh of contentment, he stowed it away, and all the difficulties of the situation were at an end.

The meal progressed peaceably with desultory conversation of no particular significance, excepting that Charlie was making himself desperately agreeable to Althea and being by no means repulsed. Presently Mr Potter addressed us jointly.

"Do either of you young people know anything about pictures and art matters in general?"

"Well, yes," said Charlie, "I suppose we do a little. We were both students at the Slade School for a time. I didn't make much of it, but Phyllis would have been quite a dab at painting if she hadn't been so beastly idle."

"The reason I ask," said Mr Potter, "is that I am getting a small collection of pictures together and I should be glad of a little expert advice."

"We aren't exactly expert, you know," Charlie remarked.

"Well, anyway, you've got some practical knowledge of painting, which is more than I have. I suppose you don't happen to have an hour or so to spare this afternoon?"

"I'm quite free," replied Charlie, blandly regardless of his "affairs," "and so, I think, is my cousin, aren't you, Phyl?"

Of course I was, and I said so, whereupon Mr Potter resumed:

"Then perhaps you wouldn't mind giving me a little help. I've got an appointment at three with an art dealer, a man named Bradley in St James' Street, who is going to show me some pictures. I believe he is quite a straight man, but still I'd be glad to have you to back me up."

We both agreed gleefully. I love buying things and so does Charlie; in fact, it was an excess of enthusiasm in this direction that caused those complications in his affairs that we were going to discuss. Accordingly, as soon as we had finished our lunch, we all trooped out and crammed ourselves into a taxi, and off we rattled to St James' Street. Mr Bradley's establishment was very quiet and select, for Mr Bradley was a great man in his way. There was no shop front or anything of that sort. It was almost like a private house, and the attendant who let us in might have been a nobleman's footman. Mr Bradley, who was a quiet, dry little man, received us ceremoniously in a large, well-lighted *salon* or gallery that seemed to be positively bursting with precious and beautiful things. Mr Potter came to the point with characteristic briskness and good sense.

You know what I have come for, Mr Bradley; I want some nice pictures to take home with me. I don't know much about pictures myself, and my friends who have kindly come to help me to choose are not professed experts. But you are. So I am going to put myself into your hands and trust you not to let me buy anything that isn't worth having."

"It's the wisest thing you could do, sir," said Mr Bradley. "No dealer wants to load up his clients with rubbish if they will only be reasonable. But I would remind you that the number of genuine Old Masters is necessarily limited, and that, of the known examples, the immense majority are locked up in public or private collections, whereas the market is flooded with forgeries."

"That sounds cheerful," Mr Potter remarked.

"Still," said Mr Bradley, "the race of painters is not extinct. Masterpieces are still being produced, and there are bona fide copies of the old works that, for decorative purposes, are almost equal to the originals. If you *will* have original Old Masters you will pay through the nose and run a big risk of getting clever forgeries. But if you will be content with modern pictures and sound copies, you can get a really fine collection at quite a reasonable price. The Old Masters were modern once, you know."

"That's true," agreed Mr Potter, "and the moderns will be Old Masters some day. Well, we'll just look at what you've got, Mr Bradley"

We walked slowly round the gallery and it became evident to me that Mr Potter, like many another inexpert picture-buyer, had a secret hankering for what Ruskin calls the "brown and shiny" type of masterpiece. But he was a man of abundant commonsense and allowed himself to be piloted safely past these doubtful and obscure antiques, though he had his own views and was not above expressing them. For instance, he was not taking on Columbus in any form.

"No," he said, after inspecting the Setting Forth, the Arrival and the Return of that doughty navigator, "I guess we're a bit fed up with Columbus. He didn't create America, anyway. He only found it and I reckon the American continent isn't the sort of thing that anyone would overlook if he happened to be passing that way. What is this Eastern subject, Mr Bradley?"

"That, sir, is 'Joseph before Pharaoh,' and a very fine picture it is. The painter, Mr Gilray, is a young man, but his reputation is growing rapidly, and he would have sold this from the walls of the Academy if he hadn't used such a very large canvas. It is really a gallery picture, but, if you have the wall-space – "

"I'll make it," interrupted Mr Potter. "I like that picture. But I don't like the frame."

"Oh, that is merely a trial frame," said Mr Bradley. "If you take the picture, it would be advisable to have a frame designed to suit the subject."

"Could you get that done for me?" Mr Potter asked.

"Certainly," was the reply. "I usually do get special frames built for important pictures unless the artist has had it done."

"Very well," said Mr Potter. "We'll consider this a deal, that is if the price is satisfactory."

The price was three hundred and fifty guineas, exclusive of the frame, and as this appeared to Mr Potter to be quite satisfactory, the transaction was closed and the procession moved on to the "next article." But my interest in John B Potter's purchases had suddenly become extinct, or rather, I should say, fulfilled. For the projected frame had shown me the way out of the difficulty that had been haunting me for days past, or at least had offered me a most luminous suggestion; and the consideration of that suggestion left me little capacity for attention to such trivialities as John B Potter or Mr Bradley's stock-in-trade. I daresay you can guess what that suggestion was, but if you can't you must just have patience until its nature appears. Meanwhile I trapsed round the gallery in a brown study, pulling myself together to say something profound whenever my opinion was asked, and wishing that John B would content himself with what he had already bought.

We bade adieu to the Potters on Mr Bradley's doorstep, after promising to dine with them on the following evening, and then Charlie took me off to a tea shop in Piccadilly to talk over his "affairs." But, bless you! he didn't care about his affairs any more than I did. All he could think of or talk about was Althea, and for that matter, I didn't blame him.

"She really is an awfully ripping girl, Phyl. She is indeed," he assured me, cramming half a crumpet into his mouth.

"Well, did I say she wasn't?" I demanded, irritably, for I was thinking about that frame.

"No, of course you didn't, but you needn't be so beastly sour about it. I'm not reflecting on you."

"Who cares whether you are or not?" I retorted (Charlie and I usually exchanged little amenities of this kind when we were together, by way, I suppose, of defining our relationship). "But," I continued, "why haven't you ever told me about her before?"

"Told you!" he exclaimed. "How the deuce could I? I never set eyes on the girl before or on John B either."

"Oh, rats!" I commented courteously.

"Rats yourself," he snarled. "I tell you, Phyl, that I never heard of those people until they came to our table at the Cheese. There's some horrid mystery about the whole affair. The fellow who picked Althea up in the Strand was not I. The Lord only knows who he was."

"But my dear Charlie, they both recognized you at the first glance!"

"I know. Chappie must have been awfully like me."

"Very," I agreed dryly. "Good-looking fellow, too."

"Oh, all right! he yapped. "I haven't taken out copyright in my mug."

"He seems to have given your name, too. How do you explain that?"

"I don't explain it at all," he replied sulkily. "I don't know who the chappie could have been, and I don't care so long as he doesn't turn up and give the show away."

I smiled a superior and sceptical smile, which so infuriated Charlie that he presently broke up the meeting and went off in dudgeon to his club. Of course this suited me to a "t." I had been longing to get rid of him and no sooner had he disappeared than I was off like a lamplighter – or perhaps I ought to say lamplightrix – to Mr Bradley's establishment in St James' Street.

The great man was still on the premises, and a little surprised, I think, to see me back, and alone, too. And I was a little disconcerted myself, for I had been in such a twitter to catch him before he left that I hadn't in the least arranged with myself what I was going to say.

"And what can I have the pleasure of doing for you, madam?" Mr Bradley asked, rubbing his hands and looking as dry as a toasted biscuit in the dog days.

Now what on earth was it that I wanted him to do? Oh, yes, of course. But it was rather difficult to explain. And he did look so horridly dry and forbidding. However, I made the plunge.

"I have been thinking, Mr Bradley – at least, that is to say, I have in a sort of way considered, though I don't know how you will regard what I was – but perhaps I am a little mistaking your – er – "

Here I turned scarlet to the tips of my ears and stared at the poor man like a stuck pig. I *must* have looked a fool.

"M' yes," said Mr Bradley.

"What I wanted you to do for me," I stammered, " is just merely – at least – well, I suppose it wouldn't be very much out of – you do take confidential commissions, I imagine?"

Mr Bradley indulged himself in a slight cough.

"I get a good many offered to me," he replied, "but I don't often accept them."

He looked at me rather severely as he said this. No doubt an art dealer has solid reasons for taking an unfavourable view of humanity, including his fellow art dealers.

"Was it something that you wished to sell?" he asked.

"No; it is something that I wish to buy," I replied.

"Ah!" he said, "that is a different matter. Pray be seated, madam, and let me hear what assistance I can render you."

His manner was so much more genial now that I had made my position comparatively clear that I was quite encouraged.

"I want you, Mr Bradley," said I, "to consider what passes between us as strictly confidential," and, as he bowed acquiescence, I continued: "Probably you are acquainted with Mr Paul Everard, the sculptor; he designs picture frames, among other things, you know."

"I have heard the name and I think I have had some frames that he designed, but I deal with the frame-makers. They employ the designer. Were you thinking of having a frame made?"

"No, not at all; it is quite a different matter. I happen to know that Mr Everard has completed a statue as far as the modelling is concerned, but can't afford to carry it any farther. It is modelled for bronze, but it has only got as far as the clay, and there it sticks for want of funds to pay the moulder and founder."

"Yes." Mr Bradley was beginning to look quite interested.

"Well, I want to buy that statue."

"Yes. But that seems quite simple. Have you made him an offer?"

"No, I haven't. You see I don't want him to know who the purchaser is."

"Oh, I see," said Mr Bradley, looking as sympathetic as a Sister of Mercy. Whereupon I immediately turned the colour of a stick of sealing-wax − red sealing-wax, I mean, of course. It is so frightfully embarrassing when people will understand you prematurely.

"Would you be willing to act for me?" I asked.

"Oh, certainly, certainly, my dear young lady," he replied, beaming on me with a sort of "Bless you, my children" expression that wasn't in the least warranted by the circumstances. "It will give me the greatest pleasure. I take it that Mr Everard is a friend of yours?"

Now I wasn't going to have him jumping at conclusions in this way, though, as a matter of fact, he had jumped pretty near the right one, so I answered as unconcernedly as I could:

"No, not a friend, nor even an acquaintance. My cousin, who was here with me just now, knows him, but he is quite a stranger to me." Which was perfectly true, if you come to think of it; for I was Miss Dudley, whereas the person who had made Paul's acquaintance was Mr Philip Rowden.

I think Mr Bradley was a little bit disappointed, but he bore up under the blow with commendable fortitude. He had sniffed a romance and he wasn't going to be lightly put off, but all the same he kept a sober eye to business.

"What is it exactly that you wish me to do, Miss Dudley?" he asked.

"Well," I replied; " I thought you might make some excuse for going to his studio – it occurred to me that Mr Potter's frame might furnish a suitable pretext – "

"Excellent! Excellent!" he exclaimed with a sly smile of approval. "The very thing. In fact I don't see why Mr Everard shouldn't design that frame. But don't let me interrupt."

"Well, then, you could go to make enquiries about the frame and you'd see the statue; you couldn't miss it as it is appreciably over life size. Then you could take a fancy to it and make an offer on your own account or on behalf of some imaginary client. But I don't mind how you manage it so long as I don't appear in the business, either to Mr Everard or anybody else."

"I quite understand," said Mr Bradley; and I really believe he did, so far as you could reasonably expect the poor old dear to understand. Naturally he could never have dreamed of Mr Philip Rowden.

"I suppose," he continued after a reflective pause, "you have considered the cost of all this? It will be a matter of some hundreds of pounds, even if Mr Everard lets the work go at a low price, as I daresay he will. You'll be pretty heavily out of pocket."

"Yes; but then I shall have the statue, you know."

"So you will," he agreed; "so you will. By the way, what are you going to do with it? A heroic-sized bronze statue isn't the sort of thing that you can put on your drawing-room mantelpiece. Have you considered that?"

Now the truth is that I had never given the matter a thought. I had been so intent on saving the clay model and letting Paul see his work in its perfect and permanent form that I had completely lost sight of everything else. But it wouldn't do to admit it, for already a slow smile was spreading over Mr Bradley's face.

"Oh," I replied carelessly, "there's no need to worry about that. I daresay I shall find some corner to put it in. How much money had I better deposit with you, Mr Bradley?"

"Let me see," he said, spreading out his fingers as counters to check the items. "We shall have to take a plaster cast from the clay, a wax model from the plaster and a bronze cast from the wax. Perhaps we can do without the plaster cast. I don't see why the founder shouldn't make his first mould from the clay direct. Even then it will be a costly affair. But perhaps I had better see Mr Everard and hear what he is willing to take for the statue as it stands. Then I can get an estimate from the founder, or from Mr Everard himself, and let you know what the whole thing will cost you."

"Thank you," I said warmly. "It is most kind of you to take all this trouble. And, by the way, you needn't drive a hard bargain with Mr Everard. It wouldn't be fair to take advantage of the difficulties of his position."

"No," he agreed; "but still, you know, Miss Dudley, you are doing a very handsome thing."

"Oh, but I think you're forgetting that I want the statue," I protested with my cheeks all aflame again. He was a little bit *too* discerning, was Mr Bradley.

"So I was," he admitted with an exasperatingly fatherly smile; "so I was. Of course you want the statue and you are willing to pay for it."

He beamed on me benevolently as he took my card from me, and when I offered him my hand, he gave it such an affectionate squeeze that I almost thought he was going to kiss me – and I'm not sure that I wouldn't have let him, he was such an old duck, and I was so awfully pleased with myself.

From Mr Bradley's I trotted homewards in a glow of self-satisfaction and brimful of delightful thoughts. Never you mind what I was thinking about. It was a highly agreeable topic if not a very novel one and its consideration kept my face wreathed in smiles of concentrated amiability; so much so that a beef-faced, over-dressed Johnnie with an eyeglass, whom I met in Pall Mall, actually smiled too. Thought I was smiling at him if you please! I could have knocked his hat off.

As soon as I got home I wrote to my stockbroker, Mr Edmonton Abbott, instructing him to sell out five hundred pounds stock, and to my bank asking to have an overdraft arranged until Mr Abbott's cheque should be paid in. This latter application I followed up next morning with a personal visit to the bank with the result that I was able immediately to deposit with Mr Bradley a sum of five hundred pounds to enable him to proceed with my commission. If there was going to be any delay it shouldn't be due to slackness on my part.

The dinner at the Savoy was quite a pleasant little function; but all the same it became very evident to me that I should have to mind my eye – if you will permit me to use the familiar colloquialism. Charlie was positively obsequious. It was so "frightfully jolly" (did you ever hear such an expression?) to have a good-looking, witty cousin to take out to dinner. Oh, yes, indeed! But I wasn't to be caught with that particular brand of toasted cheese. I saw through Master Charlie's little stratagem at a glance. Two's company, three isn't; but four – well four is a multiple of two, you see. Not that I didn't sympathize with Charlie. It was perfectly natural that he should fall in love with dear Althea. Any self-respecting young man would have done so; and Charlie, having remarkable natural facility in that direction, and having by no means permitted his gifts to dwindle for lack of exercise, had lost no time over the affair.

Nor was Althea at all insensible. Which again was natural enough. For Charlie was an exceedingly taking fellow, and good-looking, too. Remarkably good-looking (I think I have mentioned how very much alike he and I were). And Althea was just as quick as he to perceive the advantage of even numbers. It was so delightful for a stranger like her, in a strange land, to feel that she had a real girl friend. I daresay it was. But I saw plainly enough that the stranger who was going to have the society of that girl friend was John B Potter. And so did he. And, to tell the truth, he didn't seem to dislike the arrangement at all. But the rôle of "gooseberry" wasn't exactly what I was cut out for; besides, I had other fish to fry. So when the anticipated invitations were forthcoming, I became discreetly evasive.

Meanwhile the frying operations went on apace. I received a letter from Mr Bradley acknowledging my cheque and informing me that the statue had been secured for me and that a moulder had been instructed to make the preliminary cast. Which was highly satisfactory. But after that several days elapsed without bringing me any fresh news. I had no idea how long the operation of making a cast should take, but as the time ran on I began to get a little nervous and impatient. I had rather expected that Paul would write and give me the joyful tidings. Two or three times a day I crawled through into Mr Rowden's chambers to inspect the letter-box, and when I fished out nothing but moneylender's circulars and ridiculous advertisements I was ready to cry with vexation.

At length the suspense became more than I could bear. Of course it was all right, but I wanted to see for myself. No doubt Mr Bradley could have given me all the information, but the truth is I was a little shy of Mr Bradley. He was such a very discerning gentleman. Besides, I don't mind admitting that I wanted to see how Paul was taking the turn in his fortunes, especially as I hadn't seen him for quite a long time. So the end of it was that, one murky afternoon early in February, I plucked up courage to prepare for a descent on the Jacob Street studio.

It was a most providential thing that Charlie had never shown any interest in those clothes of his that were stored in my rooms. I suppose they were rather out of date, though they didn't look so to me but then I haven't Charlie's expert and fastidious eye. At any rate, there they were, despised, forgotten or rejected – most fortunately for me, for without them the existence of Mr Philip Rowden would have been seriously threatened – and I proceeded to select the most seasonable suit and make my toilette in fear and trembling lest an inopportune visitor should arrive before I had time to slip out unnoticed.

Fortune favoured me so far. Without molestation or interruption, I inducted myself into the borrowed plumage, put on my smart new hat, took my gloves and walking-stick, and, having slipped Mr Rowden's latchkey into my pocket, made a successful escape by way of the Fetter Lane gate and took my way up the murky street Holbornwards. Experience had taught me to avoid public vehicles and, as far as possible, the more frequented streets, for London holds a vast number of people, among whom were a quite considerable number of those whom I did not want to meet.

Still Fortune and the dim atmosphere of a winter's afternoon favoured me. By way of Gray's Inn and Guilford Street, Woburn Place and Euston Road, I made an uninterrupted passage as far as the middle of George Street, and was joyfully bearing down on my destination when I became aware of two men approaching from the opposite direction. In respect of one of them, an elderly, corpulent person of a strongly Semitic flavour, I was conscious of the stirring of some chord of memory – so much so that I very pointedly avoided seeing him. Swiftly and with averted face, I turned out the lockers of memory. Had I seen him before, or was this quasi-familiarity merely a reminiscence of some half-forgotten visit to the Assyrian Room at the British Museum? I was not left long in doubt. We had almost drawn abreast, and I was in the very act of slipping past, when the descendant of Shem halted dramatically and grasped my sleeve.

"Ha!" he exclaimed; "here he is. What a remarkable coincidence!"

Now this was not particularly enlightening, and it certainly wasn't true, at any rate in a strictly literal sense. But this was no time for hair-splitting. The immediate question was, "Who was I?" the further question was, "Who was he?" As to the latter, a square look into the Nebuchadnezzar-like countenance settled it. He was "Mr Shylock." I recalled his face now quite clearly, though I couldn't for the life of me remember his name. However there was no doubt that he was the original Shylock, and it followed pretty clearly that I was my cousin Charlie. As indeed appeared by his next remark.

"We were just talking about you, Mr Sidley, my partner and I – you remember Mr Campbell?"

Naturally I didn't, though I took a careful look at Mr Campbell, and thought him remarkably like Belshazzar as represented in the well-known picture. But at the moment my mind was principally engaged with the question: should I accept the honour thus thrust upon me, or should I fall back on the personality of Philip Rowden? Under the circumstances I decided to temporize.

"What were you saying about me?" I asked, having acknowledged Mr Belshazzar Campbell with a bow.

"We were wondering," replied Mr Shylock, "if you were aware that Mr Smith-Bruce had failed to meet that bill."

"Is it any business of mine whether he has or not?" I asked.

My two friends glanced at one another and exchanged Pentateuchal smiles.

"Pretty cool, that!" remarked Shylock; and Mr Campbell agreed that it was "Rather." And as I stared fatuously from the one to the other, the former added: "Considering that your name is on the back of that bill, Mr Sidley, I should think it was a good deal your business. What do you propose to do?"

"What do you expect me to do?" I asked foolishly.

"Why, I expect you to pay of course," was the reply. "But I don't want to be hard on you. Our little transactions have always been carried out satisfactorily up to the present, and I'd like them to go on the same way. If you can get hold of Mr Smith-Bruce and make him settle up, well and good. But if you can't − why, business is business, you know. I'm not going to lose my money."

"No, naturally; of course you're not," I agreed, casting about frantically for some means of escape. For it was obviously most improper for me to be listening to these details of Charlie's secret history.

"Well then, what do you propose to do?" my tormentor persisted.

I cogitated profoundly and swiftly for few seconds, and then, as if inspired with brilliant idea:

"I'll tell you what. Mr Shy − er − I'm in rather a hurry just now − "

"You generally are," he remarked.

"Yes, I know. But I have a very important engagement – "

"You generally have," said he with a Rabbinical grin, which contrived to reflect itself on the countenance of Mr Belshazzar.

"Well, at any rate," I snapped, "I can't stop now, and I'm not going to. What I was about to propose was that you should notify me of the facts in writing. You have my address, I think?"

"I should think I have. Lots of 'em. Enough to start a small directory. Which one would you advise me to write to?"

I was on the point of recommending him to write to them all, but a glimmer of prudence restrained me just in time.

"There's my club," said I, "and my old address in Clifford's Inn. That will always find me, you know. Of course," I added quickly, as he seemed about to raise some objection, "you will understand that a written statement from you will strengthen my position considerably. And now I must really tear myself away. Goodbye! Goodbye!" And before the claw which he had extended to grab my cuff could reach its mark, I had shot away and was skimming down George Street at a pace which, to the elderly and obese rendered pursuit hopeless.

As I went I reflected on what I had heard. Apparently Charlie's "affairs" were in a rather more critical state than I had supposed. By some means or other I should have to intervene, if the interesting developments in the Althea direction were not to be brought to a disastrous end – though how on earth I was to make an opportunity I could not at present imagine; and at this point I emerged into the Hampstead Road, and forthwith my own "affairs," which had fallen into abeyance for the moment, loomed up with a sudden importance that boosted poor Charles and his entanglements into the uttermost background.

As I stood on the colossal threshold of 63, Jacob Street and listened to the distant jangling of the bell, I tried to collect my thoughts and rapidly rehearse my part. Of course I knew nothing of Mr Bradley or the purchase of the statue. That must come on me as a complete surprise. It was difficult to get the position clearly into my head, muddled as I was by my late encounter and the news of Charlie's liabilities. But I should have to keep a clear brain or I was lost.

In the midst of my cogitations the sound of footsteps became audible and brought my heart into my mouth, for, odd as it may seem, I recognized them instantly. Then the wicket opened, and in a moment Paul had seized both my hands and was pulling me through the opening.

"By jove, Phil!" he exclaimed, "this is a stroke of luck. I have been going to write to you only I have been up to my eyes in work." He shut the wicket, and linking his arm in mine, piloted me down the yard, which was already shrouded in darkness.

"Yes," he continued, "I meant to write to you and I ought to have written. You're my mascot, old chap. Ever since you came here things have been looking up with me. It seems as if the tide had turned at last."

"How do you mean?" I asked rather shakily.

"You'll see in a moment," he replied. And hereupon he pushed open the door and led me into the brightly lighted studio.

I was absolutely staggered. I could have screamed aloud. The tent of waterproof cloth had disappeared and the great turn-table, whereon the clay figure had stood poised with the lightness of a disembodied spirit, was now occupied by what looked like a colossal snowman of perfectly incredible shapelessness. It is true that the creature had a sort of huge knob that might have represented a head, and it had the semblance of arms – formless, dropsical appendages that seemed to end in enormous boxing-gloves; but as to the rest, it might have been the product of a volcanic eruption save for a number of iron bars that were embedded in its stomach and elsewhere. I stared at the uncouth monster in dismay until I felt myself on the point of bursting into tears.

"Paul!" I gasped at length; "what an awful mess they've made of it!"

But he seemed to take it quite calmly.

"Think so?" he asked.

"Well, don't you?" I retorted. "Just look at it."

"What's the matter with it?" he asked.

"My," I answered, a little reassured by his tone, however, "it's so frightfully rough. It will take no end of touching up."

I gazed at him ruefully and found him regarding me with a very curious, puzzled expression and his mouth most unbecomingly agape.

"I don't quite follow you, old chap," said he. "What makes you think it will want touching up?"

"Well, look at it!" I exclaimed. "It isn't a bit like it was in the clay. I thought a plaster cast was – "

But here he interrupted me by exploding into shouts of laughter. It was awfully rude of him. I could have slapped his head.

"I don't see what there is to laugh at," I said, sourly. "You can see for yourself – "

"Why, you young lunatic," he exclaimed wiping his eyes with his apron, "that thing isn't the cast; it's the mould. The cast is inside. The workmen are coming tomorrow to chip it out, and a nice mess they'll make, confound them! But you haven't asked how I came to have the cast made."

I hadn't. In my astonishment and dismay I had forgotten that I was supposed to know nothing about the affair. I now hastened to repair the omission.

"You haven't sold the figure, have you?" I asked.

"Exactly what I have done, Phil," he answered gleefully. "I'll tell you how it happened. A few days ago, a dealer named Bradley called on me to commission a big gallery frame – I'll tell you about that later. Well, he browsed round the studio looking at the casts, and then I thought I'd show him the statue. So I did; and as he seemed mightily taken with it, I asked him – facetiously – if he'd like to buy it cheap. Of course I was only joking, but he took me up at once and fairly staggered me by offering a hundred pounds for the thing as it stood. Naturally I closed with the offer then and there, and agreed to see the thing through the founder's hands and do any retouching and finishing that might be necessary on the bronze. So the matter was settled. He wanted to have the piece-mould made direct from the clay so as to save the expense of the cast. But I wasn't going to have that to risk spoiling the clay model just to save him a few pounds. So we have had a waste-mould made, and when the cast is chipped out we shall have it to work from without any fear of failures or accidents."

"A hundred pounds doesn't sound much of a price," I remarked.

"Oh, of course it's ridiculous. But still I am only too delighted to get it. If he had offered a fiver I shouldn't have refused, for I shall see the figure in its proper material and know that it is to have a permanent existence. There is only one unsatisfactory feature in the deal."

"What is that?" I asked.

"Why, it seems that Bradley has an idea that he can plant the figure on a client of his – in fact he has a sort of commission, I gather. But he won't say who the client is or what is to be done with the statue. It looks as if the thing was likely to disappear to some unknown destination and never be seen or heard of again. That is rather a pity. Naturally, an artist likes to know where his more important works are, even if he never has a chance of seeing them. But still, an unknown foreign gallery is better than the clay-bin. Come and have a look at the frame that I was speaking of. It's for a picture of 'Joseph before Pharaoh,' and I must say that Bradley, if he was a trifle near over the statue, is treating me quite handsomely in regard to this. It's the best paid commission that I have ever had."

We crossed the studio to where the frame was set up on a sort of large easel and, as I admiringly studied the severe design, based on an Egyptian motive, Paul explained some of the technicalities.

"You see, I am working it full size in the clay so that the frame-maker can take moulds for the hard compo, in which it will have to be finally produced. I don't make the actual frame, although I shall put some finishing work on the compo while it is soft. You won't mind my going on, old chap, will you? I've promised to push it along as fast as I can."

Of course I didn't mind. On the contrary, I found it delightfully entertaining to sit on a high stool by his side and watch his deft fingers miraculously turning little pellets of clay into delicate and subtle decorative details, and I should have been well content to sit there for the rest of the day had it not been for a most alarming interruption. Suddenly the bell jangled loudly, and Paul, hastily laying down the roll of clay that he was holding, wiped his fingers on his apron and remarked:

"I expect that's Bradley. He said he might be looking in to see how I was getting on and that he would probably bring his client to look at the frame. Don't you go, Phil."

But at the mention of Mr Bradley – to say nothing of John B Potter – I had shot off my stool as if projected by a spring. It was an awful situation. One or both of them would spot me to a certainty.

"I'm afraid I must be off," I stammered, desperately hauling out my watch. "Good Lord! yes! Ought to have gone half an hour ago. But don't mind me, Paul; I can let myself out. And I'll look you up again quite soon."

There was no time to argue. Once more the bell pealed loudly and, as Paul hurried away, I followed him into the darkness of the yard. From afar off I saw the wicket gate open to admit the visitors and then on my affrighted ear fell the too familiar voices of Mr Bradley and John B Potter. I was almost at my wit's end – but not quite, for hard by was a door slightly ajar. Frantically I whisked it open and plunged into a dark cavern, which (having tripped over the wooden threshold) I ascertained beyond all doubt to be somebody's coal-cellar.

I waited motionless until the voices had passed and the studio door had shut. Then, having groped among the coals for my hat, I rose and wiped my hands on the southern aspect of my trousers – which I had learned to be the correct masculine thing to do under the circumstances. Finally, I crept up the yard on tiptoe, and having softly let myself out through the wicket, fled in the direction of Hampstead Road.

As I pursued my way home, chewing the agreeably-flavoured cud of reflection on the incidents of my visit to Paul, I found myself dwelling again and again on the anxiety that he had shown as to the final destination of his masterpiece. That anxiety seemed to me very natural. An artist creating a picture or a statue is not like a factory workman turning out a stock-pattern boot or dinner-plate, occupied only with the passing labour and indifferent to the fate of its product. To the artist, each work is part of himself, unreplaceable and never to be repeated; and naturally enough, he does not like to think of the offspring of his soul as passing for ever out of his life. I sympathized deeply with this feeling and during the next few days thought about the matter a great deal, for, of course, the fate of the statue depended on me and the question as to its destination became more acute as the time ran on.

What on earth was I to do with the thing? That was the problem to which I could conceive no solution – at least, no reasonable one. To warehouse it would hardly meet the difficulty and seemed like a mean evasion. If I gave it to some public institution – supposing anyone would have it – I should have no control as to where it might be placed or how it might be treated, and moreover, I didn't want to give it away. I wanted to keep it. If only it had been a little smaller and I could have had it in my rooms!

But still the time ran on. Then I got a very nice letter from Mr Bradley, enclosing a statement and a cheque for the balance of my deposit. The casting, he informed me, had been successfully carried out, and the finishing work done on the bronze by the artist. The statue was ready for my inspection at the premises of the founders, who were awaiting my instructions as to the address to which it was to be forwarded. All of which was very gratifying, but it reduced me to a state bordering on insanity. For still I hadn't the faintest idea what I was to do with this glorious white elephant.

And then, when I was in the very lowest depths of despair, and only prevented from tearing my hair by the impossibility of getting a fair pull at it, I had an inspiration. A noble one it was, too. It came to me in this wise. I happened to be glancing over a number of the *Studio*, and horribly bored I was, for the editor had evidently got a bad attack of Arty Craftiness and had filled up his magazine with astigmatic wallpapers, suburban villas, unsittable chairs and trash of that sort. So, finding the articles impossible, I turned for relief to the announcements and – there it was. Under the heading "Forthcoming Exhibitions," my eye lighted on the magical words: "Royal Academy. Receiving days. Sculpture, March 23."

In an instant I had bounced out of my easy chair – which wasn't an artful crafty concern at all, but just a commonplace piece of furniture designed for the sordid purpose of being sat on – whisked on my hat and coat and darted out into Fleet Street. An obliging taxi person conveyed me rapidly to Burlington House; an equally obliging secretary person furnished me with an application form and three string-tailed labels, and the taxi bore me home in triumph.

You see what my little dodge was, no doubt. I was just going to give those Academy people a chance of having something really worth looking at in their galleries for once in a way. And it was perfectly simple. By some strange chance I had kept Paul's letter, so I was able to copy his signature quite nicely. It was only when I came to fill in the address that I found myself up against a corner, as Charlie would say. But there I was regularly kyfoozled (to borrow another of his elegant expressions). It was an awful dilemma. You see my difficulty. If I put Paul's address on the form and those hanging wretches were idiots enough to refuse the statue, they would write to *him* to fetch it away, and I didn't want him to know if it wasn't accepted. And if I put my own address, and the statue was accepted for exhibition, why there it would be in the catalogue, "Paul Everard, 24, Clifford's Inn," and the cat would be out of the bag and the fat would be in the fire. It was a regular corker; it was indeed.

However, on reflection, I decided that they couldn't be such donkeys as to reject a work of that quality. Even academicians *must* know something about sculpture in spite of what the art critics say, so, in the end I boldly wrote Paul's address on the form and posted it off, and then I sent two labels to the foundry people, instructing them to affix them to the statue in the correct fashion – a stringy label to be tied to one ankle and a gummy one to be stuck on the back of the base – and to deliver the work punctually at Burlington House on the 23rd instant. Moreover, I requested them, if any enquiries were made by the artist, to say that they were acting for Mr Bradley, and on no account to mention my name.

I was mightily pleased with myself, I can tell you, but all the same I suffered the most hideous anxiety lest the foundry people should fail to deliver the work at the proper time; in fact, when the twenty-third arrived, I spent a good part of the day lurking about the alley at the back of Burlington House in a most awful twitter, until at last the masterpiece made its appearance in a large lorry, whereupon I breathed a sigh of thankfulness and departed in peace.

I have always understood that the interval between the sending-in of a work of art and the notification of the Hanging Committee's decision is a period of tribulation and anxiety. I know it was so in my case. And what made it worse was that I had no certainty of hearing the decision at all. Of course you will say that I could have looked in on Paul from time to time to see if there was any news. But I simply didn't dare to. I was in such a state of nervous excitement that I couldn't have trusted myself not to blurt out something that would have given away the whole plot.

It was a terrible time. Twice at least every day I crawled through into the chambers next door to see if there was a letter from Paul to my *alter ego*, Philip Rowden, and every time I came back with bitter disappointment in my heart and a bundle of ridiculous circulars in my hand. The suspense was wearing me to a thread. And then, at last, came my reward, in a rather qualified form it is true, but still it was better than nothing. In fact – but I had better just relate the circumstances and leave you to make any comments that may seem appropriate. It was one afternoon about the middle of April that I made my way through the loft to the next door chambers for my customary raid on Mr Rowden's letter-box; and as I had for some reason omitted my usual morning visit, I was a little extra expectant and hopeful. There were quite a lot of letters in the box, as I could see through the grating at the back, and some of them looked like private letters. In a jiffy I had the box open, and grabbing out the entire "catch," spread them out fanwise in my hand as if I were going to play Nap with them. A moment's inspection was enough. Down on the floor went the circulars, charity appeals and moneylender's "confidentials," leaving me grasping one precious missive in that comely, never-to-be-forgotten, decorative hand that I knew so well, though I had seen it but once before. With trembling fingers, I tore open the envelope and devoured the contents of the letter, standing by the open letter-box. It was quite short − Paul didn't seem to be much of a correspondent and ran thus:

"Thursday.

"MY DEAR PHIL,

"I am coming to look you up tomorrow evening at seven, and you've just got to be at home. I must see you. I am regularly up a tree and I want to consult you as to what I had better do. Be a good chum, Phil, and don't fail me.

"Yours always,

"PAUL."

I read the letter through twice and my heart sank in spite of the glow of pride and pleasure that thrilled me as I noted the value that he set on my counsel and the delightful sense of comradeship that his words conveyed. For it was perfectly easy to see what had happened. Those silly guffins at the Academy had declined his work and asked him to fetch it away, and he didn't know where to send it. Of course there was no difficulty. I should advise him to communicate with Mr Bradley, and I should write to that good gentleman myself. That was all plain sailing. But the disappointment! I could have wept. In fact I did have just to wipe my eyes a little – and got a black mark on my nose from my dusty paw. And I had made so sure of it, too! So it seemed that those art critics were right after all and the academicians were nothing but a parcel of ignorant impostors.

And, as if that wasn't enough, there was another complication. Only an hour previously I had received a telegram from that miserable young scallywag, Charlie – you really must excuse me, but surely there never was a woman since the elderly one who lived in a shoe, so badgered by her family of helpless, grown-up infants! – saying that *he* was coming to tea and that *he* wanted to consult me – "affairs" again, I supposed – and that I *must* stay in to see *him!* Of course I couldn't refuse, and of course I couldn't turn him out if he hadn't sense and good manners enough to go before seven o'clock. It was a pretty kettle of fish!

He turned up about half-past four, looking about as gay and festive as a well-slapped tomcat. Apparently Mr Shylock had been making things hum.

"Why, what's the matter, Charlie?" I asked anxiously.

"Matter!" he exclaimed. "Nothing's the matter. I only wanted to have a little talk with you, Phyl, dear." (Phyl, dear, hey? That sounded a little serious from Master Charlie. He wasn't much addicted to endearments of that sort.) "What was it that you wanted to talk about?" I asked.

"Well," he began, turning a sort of purplish red and trying to cross both his legs over one another at once, "there are several little matters that – er – that I should like to mention. For instance, there's Althea."

"What about Althea?" I enquired.

"Why, I've been and – at least she – that is to say both of us – and her father too, for that matter, have – er – you know what I mean, Phyl."

"I'm afraid I don't," I said, watching the contortions of his legs with growing anxiety.

He turned redder than ever and opened and shut his mouth two or three times in a curiously fishlike manner. Then he had another try.

"Awfully ripping girl, she is. Good sort, too. So's her father."

I had not previously regarded John B Potter in the light of "an awfully ripping girl," but I made no comment beyond a general acquiescence in Charlie's sentiments.

"So I told her," he blurted out apoplectically.

"Told her what?"

"What do men generally tell girls?" he demanded in an injured tone.

"If you ask me, I should say taradiddles, as a rule."

"Don't be a silly ape, Phyl," he remonstrated. "You know what I mean."

"I should know much better if you'd tell me," said I.

"Well," said he, "if you are so jolly dense, I've – er – well, I've spoken to her."

"I suppose you have," said I. "Conversation would fall rather flat if you didn't."

He gibbered softly and squirmed in his chair. I wouldn't have believed that a man of his experience and *savoir faire* could have behaved like such an arrant booby.

"What on earth do you mean, Charlie?" I demanded impatiently.

"Why, I mean to say – well, I've asked her."

"Asked her what?"

"Oh, you know. Asked her if it was all right O! – Pair oar – double harness – and – and all that sort of thing, dontcher know."

"And what did she say?"

"Oh, she didn't seem to think that there were any flies in the treacle. So we fixed it up; and there you are." He gave a sigh of relief and partially untwisted his legs.

"I see," said I; "it must have been a romantic interview. How does John B Potter regard the arrangement?"

"He's all right. Seemed quite pleased when I told him; the Lord knows why."

"And keeps the information to himself," I remarked. "But if you are pleased and Althea's pleased and John B is pleased, what in the name of Fortune are you pulling such a face about?"

At this question Charlie's legs suffered a slight relapse.

"I'll tell you, Phyl; may as well make a clean breast of it. I've got myself into a bit of a mess. Backed another of those beastly bills. Turned out a frost this time. Chappie let me in. So I've had to make a little trip into the Land of Goschen."

"But does that matter?" said I. "Althea has plenty of money."

"Well, what the deuce has that got to do with me?" demanded Charlie. "I'm not marrying her as a financial spec. I tell you I'm awfully sick to think that I shall be in debt when I marry."

"How much is it?" I asked.

"About three hundred. Interest works out at something like twenty per cent."

"But that's ridiculous, Charlie," said I. "You must pay that off at once. Your little income won't stand sixty pound a year interest. I shall sell out four hundred three per cents. and pay it into your bank. Will that be enough?"

At first he wouldn't hear of it. But I wasn't going to put up with any of his nonsense. Obviously he couldn't marry with a moneylender hanging on to his coat tails, and I told him so. He saw that plainly enough himself, so in the end, he accepted my little loan (at three per cent), and would have fallen on my neck if I hadn't dodged him in time.

For all practical purposes this finished our business, and I now hoped that he would take himself off. But he didn't. He stayed on and on and on until I was ready to dance with impatience. I made interminable pauses in the conversation, but he didn't mind. He just sat and looked at me with an expression of idiotic gratitude and waited for me to begin again. However, I didn't mean to let him ruin my little entertainment. I looked at the clock – it was then twenty minutes past six – and decided to give him another ten minutes, and if he hadn't gone by then – . But fortunately, at this moment, he happened to look at the clock himself and bethought him of an appointment that he had for a quarter past. That saved the situation. As his heels beat a rapid and diminishing tattoo on the stairs, I shut the door and darted into my bedroom to effect the transformation of Phyllis Dudley into Mr Philip Rowden.

I don't mind confessing that before I began the desecrating process that was to convert the feminine butterfly into the mere male grub, I cast a wistful glance at the figure that was reflected in the long mirror. If only Paul could have seen me like that! However it couldn't be helped. Regretfully I pulled off my pretty, fluffy hair – you will please remember that it was my own hair, although it was made up into a wig – and combed the underlying stubble in a masculine fashion, with a parting at the side, noting, by the way, that it was getting rather long, especially in front, and would have to be cut again if Mr Philip Rowden's career was to be prolonged. Then I got into a suit of Charlie's more reluctantly than I ever had before. For masculine clothes, though they may be all very well as a protection from the weather, simply don't exist in an aesthetic sense. Still, I made myself as presentable as I could and did it so quickly, too, that by ten minutes to seven Mr Philip Rowden was sitting in his snug little room next door, with his nerves all of a tingle and his cars pricked up for the now familiar footstep.

The whisky and cigarettes were not in evidence this time. I knew better now. Instead, a bottle of wine and a nice little pie reposed unseen in the tiny sideboard with plates and cutlery to correspond; in fact, everything was ready for a really cosy little supper like the last one of blessed memory. I don't know why I was so nervous, unless it was that I was afraid of forgetting my part and giving my little plot away, but nervous I was, though full of pleasurable anticipation, and as the time drew near I got as fidgety in my chair as Charlie had been.

On the very stroke of seven, I heard his step on the stair, and my heart leaped – and of course the rest of me had to leap, too. I had the door open almost before he had time to knock, and there he was, with both my hands grasped in his and the most delicious glow of friendship and camaraderie in those wonderful deep blue eyes.

"Good boy, Phil," he said, as I drew him into the sitting-room. "You're a young trump. I knew you wouldn't fail me. Have I put you out at all, by descending on you like this?"

"Not in the least," I replied. "I am only too delighted to see you," which was true enough, heaven knows.

"I'm glad of that," said he, "because I badly wanted a friend's counsel and although we haven't known one another very long – well, I took to you at first sight, and I think we're pretty good friends, aren't we?"

"I'm sure we are, Paul," I replied, earnestly.

"That's right. And we always shall be, I hope; and we must manage to see more of one another in future. But we'll talk of that another time. Let me tell you about this business that I hinted at in my letter. I'm in a regular fix. It's about that statue, you know."

"Oh, what about it?" I asked, bracing myself up for the confirmation of my fears.

"Well, a rather curious thing has happened. It seems that Bradley, or his mysterious client, has sent it in to the RA."

"What! Without getting your permission?" I demanded in a shocked tone.

"Yes. Rather irregular wasn't it? Especially as they must have signed my name on the form."

"What awful cheek!" I exclaimed.

"It was rather," he agreed, "though I'm not going to complain of that. Naturally I have no objection to its being in the show."

"Are they going to hang it, then?" I asked eagerly.

"I hope not," he replied with an exasperating grin. "They don't usually hang statues, you know."

"Well, exhibit it, then," I almost gasped.

"Yes, they've accepted it for exhibition. I received the notice and the exhibitor's ticket yesterday."

Here he paused to fill his pipe with deliberate care, and I sank back in my chair, completely overcome by the sudden revulsion of feeling. Excessive and unexpected joy is almost akin to pain, and plays old gooseberry with the female nervous system. I felt a sudden impulse to laugh aloud – very loud – and began to be aware of a sensation – you will understand if you are a woman, and if you aren't, it doesn't matter – as if I had swallowed a tennis ball and hadn't been able to get it down more than half way. But I kept myself in hand by shutting my lips very tightly and waited for Paul to continue.

"So it's all plain sailing so far. But that isn't all." Here he paused again to light his pipe, and I got the most awful jumps. Then he continued: "When they sent me the ticket they enclosed a letter informing me – " here he stopped to strike another match, and I nearly screamed – "informing me that – puff – puff – that the President and Council of the Academy desired to purchase the statue for the nation under the terms of the Chantrey Bequest."

I drew in my breath quickly and gripped the arms of my chair. The tennis ball was swelling rapidly and wouldn't go down for all my efforts to swallow it. Also the impulse to laugh was becoming irresistible.

Nevertheless I managed to croak out half-articulately: "How awfully jolly!" with painful consciousness of the utter banality of the remark.

"Yes," said Paul, "it's very gratifying, but also it's rather tantalizing. Of course, apart from the very flattering recognition if they bought the statue and put it in the National Collection at the Tate Gallery, my position as a sculptor would be made. *But* – if I am not mistaken, the terms of the Chantrey Bequest stipulate that the work shall be bought from the Academy Exhibition and from the artist himself. That's the difficulty. You see, the statue isn't mine, so I can't sell it."

By this time the tennis ball had grown to a football, and down it positively refused to go. And laugh I must – or cry – or both. I felt it coming, and that only made it worse.

"It seems," Paul resumed, looking at me a little queerly, "that Bradley, or his client, has priced the statue at two thousand pounds. It's a pretty good profit on a hundred, but I say nothing to that. What occurs to me is that they might possibly be induced to let me buy the statue back if I agreed to let them have the two thousand as well. If that could be managed – "

He broke off abruptly to regard me with an astonished stare, for I had suddenly begun to giggle, softly but continuously, with a sort of obligato accompaniment of sniffs.

"What's the matter, old chap?" he asked anxiously.

"Nothing, thank you," I replied, making a frantic effort to stop. But it was no go. In a couple of seconds I had begun again.

"Don't see what the devil there is to laugh at," he said, glumly.

I admitted quaveringly that there was nothing to laugh at; and then my eyes filled suddenly.

"Here, I say, don't be an ass, Phil," he exclaimed. "Pull yourself together." By way of assisting at this operation he came and thumped my back until I thought he would dislocate my spine.

"Feel better now, old chap?" he asked sympathetically.

"Yes, thank you," I gasped. "I'm quite all right now. Ha! Ha! Yoo-hoop! This last may have been a sob or a guffaw, I'm sure I don't know which it was. But the football was growing – growing – it was a pumpkin, a roc's egg, it seemed to be strangling me. In desperation I clutched at my collar and gasped for breath.

"Here, let me do that, old chap," said Paul.

His strong hands were at my throat. Away went my necktie, my collar-stud flew across the room; my collar and the neck-band of my shirt burst open and –

Well, of course, the game was up. I knew it directly I caught his eye, and felt my face turning red-hot. The cat was fairly out of the bag, and I really wasn't sorry. I had had enough of its kickings and strugglings. For, I need not remark that a girl's throat isn't at all like a man's. It's a superior sort of thing altogether, and I was rather proud of mine. And, of course, Paul, being a sculptor, was fully aware of the difference. So there it was. And the instant the catastrophe had befallen my symptoms subsided and a holy calm settled down on me.

For some seconds Paul stood gazing at me in silence. Then he said, somewhat gruffly:

"Well, I'm hanged. You're a woman, Phil, aren't you?"

There was no use denying it so I didn't try. I simply and humbly said "yes."

Well he said, "I suppose you've got some proper clothes, haven't you?"

"Of course I have," I replied. "D'you suppose I usually – "

"Well, go and put 'em on," said he. "I'm not going to talk to you in that ridiculous masquerade."

Accordingly I sneaked away, a good deal abashed, into the bedroom. There, I set up the library ladder and up I went into the loft and through into my own chambers. It didn't take me long to pick out the prettiest frock I had and put it on in place of the miserable collection of textile tubes that I had borrowed from Charlie. Then I cast a longing glance at my wig, but, of course, that was out of the question. Paul knew I had short hair. And besides, a wig is a little insecure at times, and it would be so awfully awkward if it came off at the wrong moment. However my front hair wasn't so very short, and when I had parted it in the middle and fluffed it up a little, it looked better than you'd have expected. Then I put a little lace shawl over my head and fixed it under my chin with a brooch, and really, when I looked in the glass, well, I assure you that the effect wasn't half bad. So I nipped up through the trap and made my way along the loft with a little more care than usual – though I had dusted the floor pretty thoroughly with Charlie's trousers on my previous journeys – and down I came into the bed-room of the late Philip Rowden. I was a little alarmed, for Paul had been so very gruff and short, and I didn't know what sort of a reception I was going to get. So I entered the sitting-room with downcast eyes, looking as humble as you please.

But, bless you! I needn't have troubled. The boot was on the other leg now. As I entered the room, Paul stood up as meek as Moses and looking quite nervous and shy. But I could see that he was rather struck by my appearance.

"Ah," he said, "this is a great improvement, Miss – er – Miss Rowden – your name is Rowden, isn't it?"

"No, of course it isn't," I answered.

"Oh, indeed. Then what am I to have the pleasure of calling you?"

"My name," said I "is Phyllis Dudley. Charlie generally calls me Phyl – and so do you for that matter, don't you?"

"I have done hitherto. And if we are still friends – "

"But of course we are. You said so yourself just now."

"Thank you – Phyl," said he, and then there was a slightly awkward silence, which was at length broken by his saying: "If we are just as good friends as before, Phyl, I am going to ask you a question, and you must answer me quite candidly. I have been thinking, while you have been away, and it occurs to me that you know who bought that statue. Am I right?"

"Yes," I answered.

"Well, whose property is it now?"

Of course it was no use trying to hedge, because there was that Chantrey Bequest business to settle. So there was nothing for it but to own up.

"Why," I answered, "it's your property, of course. What did you suppose? I only took it over to get it finished."

I really thought for a moment that he had caught the football disease from me, his voice was so extraordinarily queer and shaky. Still I managed to make out what he said, and very sweetly the words sounded to my ears in spite of his huskiness.

"Phyl. You are the noblest, sweetest, most generous and most sympathetic girl that ever an unworthy man had the presumption to love and worship – "

But there! There's no need for me to repeat all that he said. I have told you my story up to this without reserve, but you will understand that there are certain little tit-bits of one's autobiography that one likes to keep for one's own consumption. But I don't mind admitting to you, in confidence, that I was mighty glad that I hadn't put on that wig. For I do believe it would have come off. And what an awful anticlimax that would have been!

Of course, I am still Phyllis. But I am flighty no longer. I have sown my wild oats and gathered in a harvest of happiness beyond words. And so Phyllis the regenerate bids you adieu until we meet again; or should "Phyllis" perchance seem too familiar, I may mention that my official title is "Mrs Paul Everard," and I wouldn't change it for that of the Queen of England. So there!

R Austin Freeman

The D'Arblay Mystery
A Dr Thorndyke Mystery

When a man is found floating beneath the skin of a green-skimmed pond one morning, Dr Thorndyke becomes embroiled in an astonishing case. This wickedly entertaining detective fiction reveals that the victim was murdered through a lethal injection and someone out there is trying a cover-up.

Dr Thorndyke Intervenes
A Dr Thorndyke Mystery

What would you do if you opened a package to find a man's head? What would you do if the headless corpse had been swapped for a case of bullion? What would you do if you knew a brutal murderer was out there, somewhere, and waiting for you? Some people would run. Dr Thorndyke intervenes.

R Austin Freeman

Felo De Se
A Dr Thorndyke Mystery

John Gillam was a gambler. John Gillam faced financial ruin and was the victim of a sinister blackmail attempt. John Gillam is now dead. In this exceptional mystery, Dr Thorndyke is brought in to untangle the secrecy surrounding the death of John Gillam, a man not known for insanity and thoughts of suicide.

Helen Vardon's Confession
A Dr Thorndyke Mystery

Through the open door of a library, Helen Vardon hears an argument that changes her life forever. Helen's father and a man called Otway argue over missing funds in a trust one night. Otway proposes a marriage between him and Helen in exchange for his co-operation and silence. What transpires is a captivating tale of blackmail, fraud and death. Dr Thorndyke is left to piece together the clues in this enticing mystery.

R Austin Freeman

Mr Pottermack's Oversight

Mr Pottermack is a law-abiding, settled homebody who has nothing to hide until the appearance of the shadowy Lewison, a gambler and blackmailer with an incredible story. It appears that Pottermack is in fact a runaway prisoner, convicted of fraud, and Lewison is about to spill the beans unless he receives a large bribe in return for his silence. But Pottermack protests his innocence, and resolves to shut Lewison up once and for all. Will he do it? And if he does, will he get away with it?

The Mystery of Angelina Frood
A Dr Thorndyke Mystery

A beautiful young woman is in shock. She calls John Strangeways, a medical lawyer who must piece together the strange disparate facts of her case and, in turn, becomes fearful for his life. Only Dr Thorndyke, a master of detection, may be able to solve the baffling mystery of Angelina Frood.

'Bright, ingenious and amusing' – *The Times Literary Supplement*